His hand was firm on her arm.

"It is a matter of urgency that you tell no one you saw me last summer at your estate."

Cornelia watched him coolly. "Urgency? Forgive me, milord, if I find it passing difficult to believe you." In light of the discovering of her husband's deceptions, it was hard for Cornelia to have faith in any man. "As for the intrigue in which you are quite obviously embroiled, I do not wish to know anything more about it."

His hand on her upper arm tightened enough to remind her that he might be dressed like a harmless dandy, but he had the strength of two men. There was nothing of the fop in his bearing now. If anything, he was all raw virility and confidence.

LADY FAIR

Rebecca Ashley

FAWCETT CREST · NEW YORK

Chapter 1

The musicians were a noisy group as they maneuvered their harps and basses and violins down the hallway. It was evening. Although Cornelia had been busy all day, there was still much that had to be done. She needed to show the musicians where to set up the instruments in the back room. She also must talk to the pastry chef she had imported from London for the occasion. He was showing himself to be quite temperamental, with the consequence that the rest of the kitchen staff was close to mutiny. Cornelia made a further mental note to speak with the man in charge of setting up the tables and booths in the yard. Those were the things foremost in her mind. A host of other things awaited her attention.

Cornelia ticked some of those things off on her fingers as she stood in the entryway, her tall figure looking insignificant at the edge of the immense stone room. She gave up using her fingers to count the thousand details and used them instead to push back the thick brown curls tumbling across her forehead.

"First the musicians," she said aloud to no one in particular.

She was on her way toward the back room to see to them when the butler approached her. Stiff in his seldom-worn scarlet livery, and pigeon-breasted with authority, he announced, "A gentleman is here to see you, milady."

She cast a distracted glance at the servant. "Who is he?"

"The gentleman would not give me his name." He cleared his throat uncomfortably, "Actually, he asked to speak with Sir Frederick, but when I told him of the—the misfortune, he requested a meeting with you."

It was indeed strange for someone to call for her husband. Certainly everyone in this part of the country knew the fate that had befallen him. Quite aside from the shock of someone appearing and asking to see Frederick was the very real matter that Cornelia had no time for unexpected visitors.

She was in the last-minute stages of preparation for the fair that would begin tomorrow. Guests had already begun arriving, and there was still much to be done. At the same time, she was curious about this person who had come to call on her husband three months after his death. The visitor could not possibly be a friend, or he would have known of the accident. And why wouldn't he give his name to the butler?

"Please show him to the gray room," she said. "I'll be there directly."

It was closer to fifteen minutes before Cornelia was finished with the disorganized musicians. She entered the gray room with her black skirts rustling. Named for its pearly granite walls, the gray room was another of the massive rooms that had been built during medieval times when the castle had served more as a fortress than a home. Until the large bay windows were added to this room three years ago, the only windows had been narrow slits in the walls designed to keep arrows out.

Cornelia's gaze went immediately to the tall, almost strapping, man who stood gazing up at a portrait of her. "I'm Lady Devenish," she announced briskly. Her voice, which was always low for a woman, was now husky with breathlessness.

The man turned toward her, then glanced back at the portrait. She had sat for the painting at her most formal, with her dark brown hair carefully arranged into curls and her nutmeg brown eyes looking proudly out at the world. The green satin gown was one of her favorites, but, of course, she could not wear it now that she was in mourning. The picture made her look somber and older than her four-and-twenty years.

The stranger bowed formally to her. "Please forgive my intrusion, ma'am. I am Edwin Sorrels."

His carefully chosen, polite words surprised her. From his tanned skin and well-developed muscles she had judged him one who labored for his living. His clothes were serviceable but scarcely of distinctive quality. His accent, she noted, did not have the polish of London, but it did bear traces of some tutoring in his remote past. She suspected he was a village squire.

"I came to see Sir Frederick." He paused before continuing carefully, "Your servant said your husband had met with misfortune."

The stranger seemed to be waiting for her to confirm this. "Yes, Frederick was killed three months

3

ago by a highwayman." Cornelia could finally say the words without bursting into tears. When the constable had first come to her with the news Frederick had been murdered, she had crumbled in sorrow. Her husband of four years and the father of her infant daughter could not possibly be dead, she had insisted. For days she had clung to that belief. Gradually reality had set in, although there were still times she found it hard to believe she was a widow.

Aware of the silence in the room, she asked, "May I inquire how you knew my husband?" More to the point, why had he come to see him? she wondered.

"We met in London."

"London," she repeated in surprise. "Frederick scarcely ever went there."

"It was some time back. At Tattersall's, while we were both looking at horseflesh, I believe. Or possibly it was elsewhere."

His vagueness disappointed her. She continually wanted to talk about Frederick with people who had known him.

Edwin Sorrels glanced out the window where tables and booths for the fair were being constructed on the broad lawn. Her husband's family had begun the event over three hundred years ago. It had started as a cattle fair, but the tradition continued today as a pleasure fair held every Midsummer Eve and lasting for five days. Even though Cornelia was deep in mourning, she had been determined to hold the fair. She knew Frederick would have wanted her to continue the tradition.

"Was the highwayman ever apprehended?" the stranger asked.

Cornelia looked down at the oriental swirls in the

carpeting. "No," she said in a barely audible voice. Thinking of the man who had killed her husband still upset her. Her Frederick had been so good and trustworthy. What manner of man would have callously taken his life?

"Did anyone else see the highwayman or get his description?" Edwin Sorrels asked.

"There was a boy present, but he was terrified and could tell us little." Frustratingly little, Cornelia recalled.

Still, there had been a great effort to find the man. The constable had gone out with a party of men to search the hills around the estate and all the way to Plymouth. He had found nothing.

The stranger watched her intently. "The boy is still in your employ?"

Cornelia stared at the tall stranger, resentment beginning to build. Who was he to come to her house asking her upsetting questions? He said he was a friend of Frederick's, but she had never heard her husband speak of him. Besides, any man of delicacy would not have pressed her in this matter.

Edwin Sorrels must have guessed her thoughts, for immediately he said, "I beg your pardon, ma'am. I have offended you with my rude questions. Pray forgive me."

She inclined her head stiffly in acknowledgment. As her gaze swept over him again, she noticed things she had missed before. Dried mud coated his boots and lines of fatigue etched furrows into what she suddenly realized was a not unhandsome face. Where was her sense of duty? He was a visitor; common courtesy dictated that he be offered refreshment and shelter. "You must be tired," she said. "Have you had a long journey here?"

"From London."

London. No wonder he looked tired. "I shall order your carriage seen to immediately."

"There is no carriage. I rode my horse."

Dear heavens, he must be exhausted. He should be shown to a room immediately. But she had no free rooms. Besides, she had the oddest sense about this man—as if there were things about his visit still unsaid. The fact remained, however, that he had made a long trip to see her husband. The very least she could do was offer him a night's lodging.

Unfortunately, this was the worst possible time to have an additional houseguest. "Naturally, you are welcome to stay," she said. "I regret that the accommodations may have to be makeshift."

"Yes, I see that you are busy." Again he glanced toward the bay window. Cornelia watched how his body moved as he turned. In spite of his size, he had the litheness of a cat. "I shall not intrude on your hospitality long," he assured her quietly.

Nodding, she walked to the corner of the room to ring for the footman.

Edwin Sorrels crossed to her side. Cornelia looked at him curiously. She was tall for a woman, but he was taller than she, so she had to look up to see into his eyes. She sensed there was more he wanted to say, but he was not sure how to proceed.

"Is there something more?" she asked.

"Yes." He cleared his throat. "I have something Frederick left with me the last time we saw one another. I think it only proper that I return it to you." He reached into his pocket.

Cornelia went cold. The object he held toward her was a gold filigreed case. He opened it, and she stared at the painted miniature of herself. She had

6

given it to Frederick before he left on a trip to his other estate in Cornwall. She had been with child at the time, and she had asked him not to go. That had been right after Britain returned to war with France, and she had been nervous about him being near the coast, even on the western shore of England.

Frederick had gone anyway and had returned a month later looking strained and unhappy. He had lost her miniature, he told her. Now here it lay in the palm of a man she had never seen before.

"Where did you get this?" she asked thickly.

"From Frederick. In London."

Cornelia looked directly at Edwin Sorrels. His eyes were a more vivid shade of green than she had realized, she noted as she studied his face closely in search of further clues about him. His clothes might be simple, but she could see intelligence in his face. And cunning? Why did she still feel there was much about his visit that was a mystery?

"I believe we were at the tables at the time," Edwin added.

"I see." But she didn't see at all. Why would Frederick have gamed with such a personal thing? Her husband had never lacked for money, and he had seldom been so deep in his cups that he would have thoughtlessly gambled away her miniature.

"Here," Edwin said.

He placed the miniature in the cup of her nerveless palm. Then he carefully curled her fingers around the tiny object. His hands felt warm and large on hers, and she sensed he meant to be comforting. The return of something that had belonged to Frederick made her emotional. Cornelia quickly moved away from him, holding herself with a dignity that gave no hint she was fighting back tears.

The butler appeared at the doorway in answer to her summons.

"Please show Mr. Sorrels to the Walnut suite." Her brusqueness covered the quiver in her voice.

The servant blinked and remained rooted to the spot. "The Walnut suite, milady?"

"Yes." She turned away. As soon as she heard the door close behind the two men, she sank into a chair. Was she mad? She had just given her husband's bedroom to a man who had raised as many questions in her mind as he had answered. But the miniature confused her. Frederick had told her he had lost it. The stranger told another tale. It had never occurred to Cornelia before that her husband had not been truthful.

One of the reasons she had married Frederick was because she had trusted him utterly. It was true that he had been a baron and his family far older and more influential than hers. But that had not been what had decided her to accept him. She had married him because she had believed that he would never let her down. Cornelia knew the pain that came with having loved someone and being betrayed. At seventeen she had been blindly and passionately in love with a man who had turned her head with grand promises but had soon left her for another. She had vowed then that she would never marry until she was absolutely certain of her intended's honesty. With Frederick, she had been certain.

The stranger was lying, Cornelia decided. She could not guess how he came to possess the miniature, but she was curious enough to want to observe

8

Edwin Sorrels more closely. There were things here she would like to understand better.

Baby Elizabeth was just waking when Cornelia reached the nursery. Taking the eight-month-old in her arms, Cornelia sat in the chair by the window and loosened her clothes to free a breast.

"It's outrageous for a woman of your birth to nurse your own baby," her friends had objected. "That's what wet nurses are for."

Cornelia had ignored them. From the very beginning, she had wanted to hold her baby, to touch and to feed her. Everything about the tiny girl had seemed perfect. Cornelia would have been content to sit for hours and simply stare at the child.

Immediately after Frederick's death, she had done just that. She had ignored the demands of running a large household to be with her daughter. The only time she could be persuaded to leave was when someone needed her skills as an herbal practitioner to make a draught or a poultice.

Gradually, however, Cornelia had forced herself to return to her day-to-day chores. After all, she told herself, it would little benefit her daughter for her to let the estate languish.

Elizabeth finished nursing, and Cornelia put the baby girl up on her shoulder and patted the tiny back. Through the chintz curtains on the window she could see white clouds in a blue sky. She felt very serene as she began to hum aloud.

"Ah, I thought I would find you here."

Cornelia looked toward the door as her mother-in-law entered. The dowager was also a tall woman. An overbite kept her from being handsome, but she had a grace of carriage that made her stand out in a crowd.

"You'll spoil that child with so much attention," the older woman scolded.

Cornelia bit back a sigh. She had always taken pains to keep her relationship with her mother-in-law cordial. Of late that had not been easy. The shock of Frederick's death had made his mother unpredictable and often difficult. "I only came in a few minutes ago," Cornelia said.

"Well, I daresay you've earned a bit of peace," the dowager relented. "Have all the houseguests arrived?" She sat on a nearby chair and worked her fingers restlessly.

The mood was broken, and Cornelia no longer felt so serene. "Your cousins from Exeter are not yet here, and the Devenishs from Wales have sent word they will be delayed a day." Cornelia arranged the baby more comfortably on her shoulder before adding, "I have had one unexpected guest. His name is Edwin Sorrels. He knew Frederick."

"Sorrels? Is he connected to the Sorrels of Kent? They were all rather slight and pale-looking as I recall."

Cornelia thought of the tall, stalwart man with the glow of health on his skin and was sure there was no connection. She shook her head.

"One of Lord Crawford's daughters married a Sorrels," the older woman continued.

It had not occurred to Cornelia that the visitor might be married. Not that she cared in the least. After all, she was not looking at men. She had been a widow only a few months. But she was guiltily aware that she had noted his handsomeness and the vividness of his forest green eyes.

"I don't believe he is connected with the Craw-fords, either. I daresay his connections don't signify for he won't be staying long. Only a day or so I should imagine."

The dowager nodded, her interest already wan-dering. Rising, she began to pace the long, narrow room. "You have not forgotten anything regarding the fair, have you? It is important that all go well."

"All is arranged," Cornelia assured her. She had been giving her the same assurance these three weeks past.

"And you are prepared to give the welcoming speech tomorrow?" her mother-in-law pressed.

"Yes." The thought of standing in front of a crowd and speaking terrified Cornelia, but she was resolved. Everything Frederick would have done, she intended to do. Theirs had been a marriage of mutual support; now that he was gone she wanted to serve his memory proudly.

The dowager stopped pacing and stood over Cor-nelia. "The baby is asleep. Why don't you put her down? You look as if you are half-asleep yourself. You should go to your bed."

"I believe I will."

Cornelia *was* tired, but once in bed she did not doze. Ever since Frederick's death, she had slept poorly. Lying beneath the flowered canopy, she gazed up from her pillow and reflected that no sleep at all was preferable to the dreams she often suf-fered.

In her dreams she was sitting beside Frederick in the carriage. The light of the moon was blocked by the heavy growth of trees, just as the boy had described it. Cornelia saw the door of the carriage being wrenched open and saw the shadowy form of

11

a man in the doorway. She watched him raise a pistol and shoot.

Sitting helplessly, she watched her husband falling, falling, falling. Blood poured from the wound near his heart.

She always awoke from that dream feeling frightened and helpless and chilled. Deliberately she forced her thoughts to other things. What came immediately to mind was the fair.

After Frederick's death, she had been too perturbed to see to the plans personally. The result was that the estate overseer and his sweet but simple wife had made many of the arrangements. When she finally was able to turn her attention to helping them, Cornelia had been dismayed to learn they had engaged a "Learned Pig" and a "Fireproof Lady" who dipped her hands into boiling oil. That was not the worst of it. In the Great Booth, a play called the "Hall of Death" was to be staged with a cast consisting solely of dwarfs.

Turning restlessly in bed, Cornelia consoled herself with the thought that at least she had canceled the cock fighting and bear baiting. But because she had been unable to engage actively in the plans until little more than two weeks ago, it had been too late to change some things.

She would make the best of it this year and arrange a more respectable fair next year, she consoled herself. Surely the guests, most of whom were Frederick's relatives, would understand if things were not as well managed this year. Many of them thought she should not even undertake the task of the fair at all.

Firm in the conviction she was doing the right thing, Cornelia finally slipped into sleep.

This night she did not suffer any unhappy dreams. She awoke clear-eyed and energetic, ready for the opening day of the fair.

Clad in only her chemise, she spent a few moments looking out the window of her spacious bedroom. Her window had a view over the herb garden at the back of the house. Further away she could see the corner of the ancient stone tithe house. In the pasture she saw a groom out exercising the horses.

The manor house itself sat atop a small rise in an area blessed with a rare form of green stone known as Hurdwick stone. Even in winter the hills around the area looked green. But it was not winter now. A fresh summer breeze blew in through the open window. She would have been content to linger here and enjoy the view and the feel of the air. But duty beckoned.

With a sigh of resignation, Cornelia called for her maid.

Her maid Beth was a young Irish girl who assisted her into a black muslin gown with a square, prim neckline. Cornelia's figure had not quite returned to its former size since the birth of the baby; she was compensated for this by the increase in the size of her bosom. Her coloring had changed as well, so that her normally pale skin was infused with delicate roses on the cheeks.

The maid brushed Cornelia's brown hair until it shone. Then she wove a necklace of black beads through the curls. Cornelia paid little attention to the maid's work. Her stomach was clenched in apprehension. In a few moments she would have to go out before the crowd already gathering near the front of the house and give the welcoming address.

13

"I'm nervous, Beth," she confided.

"Tsk. Not a bit of it, ma'am. You will do just fine."

Would she? For the last four years Cornelia had stood beside Frederick on the steps of the ancient stone house while he welcomed villagers, houseguests, fair people, tradesmen, and even the gypsies loitering on the edge of the crowd. The gypsies' ancestors had been coming to the fair ever since it began, so they were as much a part of the event as the races that would be held tomorrow.

Now Frederick was dead and it was up to Cornelia to stand in front of all those people and speak.

Beth nudged her gently. "It's time, ma'am."

"Yes, of course." Rising, she took a deep breath and started out of the room. Her courage wavered as she headed down the steps that hugged one side of the wall of the great hall. At the bottom step, she paused. Through the open doors she saw the crowd. There were so many people. Dear Lord . . .

The dowager came up beside her. "Go along," she said smartly. "We must not keep our guests waiting."

Cornelia took a step toward the door and then another, fighting down an urge to bolt back up to her room.

Then she was outside standing on the top step. The servants stood behind her in stiff lines, the houseguests were seated in front of her in the few rows of benches that had been erected. Behind them stood the rest of the fairgoers. Cornelia swallowed nervously and looked around. She saw men leaning out of booths to listen and women standing in the open space in the center of the fairgrounds. A hush fell over the crowd at her appearance.

She wet her lips. "I-I-It's so good to have all of you here." Her words were little more than a whisper. People leaned forward, straining to hear.

Cornelia wiped her damp hands on the side of her skirt. "I w-w-want to w-welcome you to our festival."

The words had rung with excitement and conviction when Frederick had said them. People had cheered him. Her weak proclamation was met with polite silence.

She cleared her throat and began delivering the short, much-rehearsed speech. Amazingly, she remembered most of the words she had repeated so often in the silence of her room. The words tumbled out faster than she wanted them to, and there was a quake in her voice, but at least she was able to speak. "... I am glad that you have come." She paused to draw breath. Someone in the first row applauded, and others followed suit.

Nodding, she continued nervously, "As always, we will have plays and amusements. I hope you will enjoy yourselves. There is free ale today but pray do not imbibe overmuch."

A scattering of laughter met this announcement. "Thank you," she finished.

Her legs felt limp as people began to rise. The musicians struck up a tune on the lawn at the side of the house. Archers headed toward the field behind the tithe barn where the archery contest would commence in half an hour. In the great quadrangle that was the heart of the fair, people were already beginning to haggle with merchants and to gossip with neighbors. The houseguests crowded around Cornelia.

"You were splendid, dear," Hortense, a raw-boned second cousin of Frederick, lied firmly.

"Quite remarkable," the urbane Sir Cedric agreed, flicking a speck of dust from his waistcoat.

Cornelia murmured her thanks. She had vague impressions of guests mingling with each other in the great hall. Her hands still shook, and her legs were unsteady. She saw Edwin Sorrels standing alone beside a stone pillar watching the other guests. He probably didn't know anyone here, she realized, and used that excuse to escape from the crowd and proceed over to his side.

"I should explain to you about our fair, Mr. Sorrels." Cornelia spoke rapidly, still full of nervousness. "It is the custom that rank means little during fair time. For the next five days the houseguests will be treated like the people on the lawn. Oh, there will be some banquets in the evenings for the guests," she hastened to add, "but the rest of the time you must feel free to join in the games and to have your palm read by the gypsies and to watch the Mumming Plays."

"Thank you." He smiled at her. It was a gentle smile, probably calculated to calm her.

It didn't work. She sensed an underlying tension between them. Edwin Sorrels looked honest enough, but there were things about him she did not know, particularly about his acquaintance with Frederick. Now was an excellent opportunity to find out. "Where did you say you hailed from, Mr. Sorrels?"

"Cheltenham. Well, near there," he amended. "I scarcely think you would have heard of the hamlet where I was born."

"Do you own property there?"

"A modest amount."

So he was a landowner. He had the tanned, muscled look of a man who labored in the fields along with his tenants, if, indeed, he was wealthy enough to have tenants. His clothes suggested a rather genteel poverty. Why would Frederick have known this man? The two were clearly from dissimilar backgrounds. Her Frederick had gone to Eton. She was certain Edwin Sorrels had never passed through those exclusive halls. Frederick had liked to read and study literature. Edwin Sorrels had the look of a man who passed his free time out in the open air riding.

The dowager swept up beside her. "Cornelia, you must look to your other guests." Her glance at Edwin Sorrels made it plain she considered him of less importance than the other visitors.

Cornelia knew that arguing would be pointless and in poor taste. Still, she was embarrassed that Frederick's mother should make this man feel so unimportant. She added a softening smile as she turned to him and said, "Excuse me, please."

As she took her leave from him, her curiosity was far from satisfied.

Chapter 2

By late afternoon the crowd was beginning to feel the effects of the ale. Many of the men sat in groups beneath the yews that formed a border around the great quad and sang boisterous songs. Children, tired from the long day, ignored the antics of the joker circulating through the crowd and bickered with each other. Few people paid much attention to the blond-haired woman wearing a black dress and a tall pointed hat adorned with figures of stars and the moon as she walked onto the stage.

Suddenly and dramatically she snatched flames from the air. Silence fell abruptly and all eyes fastened on her. Moving across the stage with sinister grace, she discovered butterflies in her sleeve. She released the silvery-winged butterflies into the darkening sky. Children in the front rows stood to bound after them but froze as the mystery woman made a dog sing. Then she parted a chain's locked links with a casual wave of her hand.

Standing in the shadow of an ancient oak, Edwin watched people in the crowd as much as he watched the performer. He paid particular attention to the man in faded breeches who leaned against the lime tree and to the man with the white beard who sat on the ground near the stage.

And then there was Frederick's widow. She sat in the front row with her daughter on her lap. The severity of her black gown made her hands and face look even paler and more fragile. Her eyes were wide in the oval of her face.

She was not what Edwin would have guessed had he ever thought about it. Lady Devenish seemed unable to hide her feelings behind those wide brown eyes. He could read every emotion that flitted across her face, especially her suspicion of him. She was comely enough although not striking. Except when she smiled, he amended. Her smile revealed beautiful white teeth and brought life to her eyes. Pity she smiled so seldom.

He had paid close attention to her during the course of the day. At times she looked lost, as indeed she must feel. As a new widow with a small child and no male in the family to offer protection, hers was not an easy lot. But that was no concern of his. He had far weightier matters on his mind.

The news of Frederick's death had changed everything. It put Edwin at a loss as to how to proceed. He didn't doubt that he would think of something—he was known to be resourceful—but for the moment he admitted to frustration.

The audience erupted into applause, and Edwin glanced back toward the stage. The lady sorcerer was leaving, he noted, and quietly he moved from the shadow of his tree. He made his way into the undergrowth at the far edge of the grassy quadrangle. Edwin was used to navigating in the dark and was little slowed by the darkness or the briars or the uneven ground. Surely and steadily he made his way to the pond and waited at the edge of it.

A moment later the woman was beside him.

She greeted him with a grave nod. "Does anyone here know you?" was her first question.

"No," he replied. "These are people who seldom come up to London."

"Good."

Both fell instantly silent at the sound of a noise. "It was only a fish breaking the water," he said.

"Yes." She had discarded the black hat, he saw. She looked older than on stage. "You must already know that Frederick is dead, Natale."

"Yes, but I had no way of getting the word to you. Besides, it was still important that you come to the fair."

"You must try to find out who killed him." He handed her a purse heavy with silver. "That should be enough to loosen some tongues. I know a boy who was with Frederick at the time he was killed. I will try to coax something out of him. You must use the money to try to buy any information you can. Be careful."

"Of course."

It was a needless comment. Natale was far too clever to endanger herself or anyone else.

"Have you talked to the widow?" Natale asked. "Perhaps she knows something."

Edwin shook his head. "I am inclined to doubt it, but when I find the right moment I will try to question her."

"She looks so vulnerable," Natale murmured. "It makes me very sad." Then she slipped the purse into a voluminous pocket of her sorcerer's gown. "I will do what I can. I must go now." She disappeared into the undergrowth with ghostly stealth.

The revelry continued in the yard long after Cornelia had retired to her room. She had had a full day. After her opening speech, she had watched the puppet show with Elizabeth. Then they had eaten, and afterward she had watched the joker turn somersaults about the great hall. Later in the afternoon, Cornelia joined the dowager and ladies of the neighborhood in a ladies' feast. Finally she had returned to the lawn with her daughter to see the witch perform.

Instead of being exhausted, she lay in bed fully alert. She wished Frederick were here so that she could discuss the day's events with him. She missed the moments of companionship they had shared late in the evening. If only he had not gone out that dark night to meet with the squire over some trifling matter that could surely have waited. If only he had taken the other road back. If only . . .

She turned restlessly in the big, empty bed. Such thoughts were pointless. Frederick was dead, and no amount of regret would bring him back. Refusing to indulge her urge to cry, Cornelia turned again on the bed.

She was drifting toward sleep when she heard a noise in the sitting room between her bedroom and the room that had been Frederick's bedroom.

Cornelia tensed. There was the sound again. Someone was moving quietly about the sitting room. Edwin Sorrels was staying in Frederick's bedroom, but he had no access to the sitting room because she had locked the door from her side. She raised up on her elbows and heard the faint sound of wood on wood, as if a drawer were being pulled open.

Her heart was thumping loudly as she pushed back the covers. She lowered her bare feet until they touched the cool wood floor.

Rising, Cornelia moved cautiously toward the sitting room. At the door she bent and looked through the keyhole. All she saw was blackness. The person in the next room did not have a light. Who would prowl about in the sitting room in the dark? Fully alarmed, Cornelia straightened and started for the hall door. Just then the sitting room door opened into her room.

She shrieked.

"Hush! You'll raise the house."

"M-Mr. Sorrels, what are you doing here?" She backed away a fearful step. She knew almost nothing about this man, and now he was standing in her bedroom.

Either he saw more clearly than she in the darkness, or he was lucky, for his hand reached out and closed securely and unerringly around her wrist. "Wait. I would have a word with you." His voice gentled. "Don't tremble so. I mean you no harm."

His words did nothing to calm her. "Then why don't you let go of me?" she asked plaintively.

He did, but she sensed he stood ready to stop her should she try to leave.

"If it's money you seek, I'll give you what I have in my reticule." Her voice still wavered.

"I'm not looking for money."

"What do you want?" The possible answer to that question terrified her. What if he had come with the intention of violating her? He was far stronger than she; she would be powerless against him.

22

"I want to talk to you," he said calmly.

She heard him move about her room until he found a candle beside her bed. He lit it.

By the first flickering pieces of light, Cornelia noted thankfully that he was fully dressed. For herself, she wore a thick cotton nightgown that revealed nothing of her figure. Still, it was unthinkable to be alone with him in her bedroom at this hour. It was also alarming.

He walked over to her and looked intently down at her. Her heart drummed faster against her chest.

"What happened to Frederick's personal effects after his death?" he asked.

Cornelia stared at him, her wide brown eyes unblinking. The question startled her. Braver now that there was light in the room, she asked, "What difference can that make to you?"

"Frederick had something of mine," he said evenly. The penetrating green eyes never left her face.

"Are you suggesting Frederick *stole* something from you?" Her voice grew thick with disbelief. "My husband was the most honest man who ever lived. He never deceived anyone, and he certainly never took anything from anyone."

"I didn't say he took it," Edwin Sorrels said patiently. "I gave it to him for safekeeping. Now I want it back."

He was lying, Cornelia decided. Frederick would have told her if he was keeping something for someone else. Frederick had told her everything. She was not going to let this stranger violate her husband's memory by so much as touching his personal possessions. "I burned my husband's things after his death," she lied brazenly.

23

He watched her in silence. She didn't think he believed her, but he finally bowed his head in acknowledgment. "I see. I'm sorry to have troubled you. Pray forgive me." He left.

Cornelia locked the door loudly behind him.

She climbed back into bed, thumped the pillow angrily, and blew out the candle. But sleep was impossible. How absurd to claim that Frederick had something of his. Ridiculous.

More to the point, it was unpardonable for the stranger to snoop in her house. Tomorrow she would ask him to leave, she resolved, as she pounded the pillow into a more comfortable shape.

Another thought pushed into her mind. It was of the miniature that Edwin Sorrels had returned to her. If he had come by it as he had said, then Frederick had *not* told her everything. Cornelia brushed that heresy aside. Of course her husband had told the truth.

And yet the miniature ... And now Edwin Sorrels claimed that he had given something to Frederick.

She pushed the doubt aside. If there were unanswered questions, they concerned Edwin and not her husband. She didn't trust the stranger, and she did not want him in her house any longer. Tomorrow she would tell him he must leave.

At length she slept.

Dawn came gently the next morning. Cornelia awoke at 5:00 AM. Rising quietly, she stole up to the third floor nursery and returned to her bed with the sleeping baby. She lay in calm silence until the sunlight shafting across the bed awoke her daughter.

"Good morning, my dear little Elizabeth," Cornelia murmured.

The baby smiled.

Cornelia tickled the tiny feet, and the baby laughed.

Cornelia laughed, too. All day yesterday she had smiled politely at arriving guests, and she had laughed obligingly at the appropriate moments. But she had felt no gaiety or happiness. Lying in bed with her daughter, she felt happy. If only Frederick were here, everything would be perfect.

As happened every morning, she was saddened by the first full realization of the day that she was a widow. She tried to shake the thought aside. She could not dwell on her grief. Not during the fair and while she had a houseful of company. Already she heard guests passing in the hall outside her door.

"I should go downstairs and join them for breakfast," she whispered to the baby.

Elizabeth cooed back at her.

In the end, Cornelia chose spending time with her baby to joining the houseguests. As a consequence, she did not see Edwin Sorrels again until almost noon. When she did see him, it was at the racetrack behind the ruins of the old Norman church. Cornelia was seated in the front row of the wooden stands waiting for the race to begin. Edwin Sorrels stood beside an elderly man on the grass in the center of the racetrack.

Seeing him reminded her again of last night's incident and rekindled her anger toward him. As soon as the race was over, she would summon her uninvited guest to her parlor and tell him to leave.

Her attention was diverted from Edwin Sorrels as the race began. The horses were sleek and well groomed; their coats shone in the sunlight as they pounded around the track with riders clinging to their backs. It soon developed into a close contest between two fierce lead horses. First one would pull ahead and then the other.

People in the stands leaned forward excitedly and shouted their encouragement. In the center of the course, the crowd edged forward until some people stood close enough to feel the spray of foam from the horses' mouths.

"Look," someone shouted.

Cornelia turned her gaze to a man who was moving onto the track. His walk was hobbled, and he smiled mindlessly. He began waving at the crowd. He was an idiot, she realized. She looked anxiously down the track and saw the horses thundering toward him.

Others saw the danger, too. Women screamed and averted their eyes, and men yelled for the hapless man to get out of the way. A couple of people darted out of the crowd to grab him but had neither the speed nor daring to venture all the way to the center lane where the idiot stood waving. Then she saw Edwin Sorrels break through from the crowd. He ran to the man, grabbed him by the neck and flung him to the ground at the edge of the track. The last thing Cornelia saw before the horses obstructed her view was Edwin Sorrels throwing himself atop the confused man.

The outcome of the race was ignored in the scramble to help the two men.

Cornelia said a quick, fervent prayer that they were uninjured, then rose unsteadily and made her way out of the stands. The crowd was oblivious to her, and she had to shoulder her way through.

She reached the center of the drama in time to see Edwin Sorrels shaking himself out of the hold of two overzealous caretakers.

"I'm fine," he said brusquely and dusted at his clothes.

It was a hopeless gesture. His shirt was torn from the elbow to the shoulder, revealing a rippling expanse of tanned muscles that gleamed with a sheen of sweat and some blood. His breeches were dark with packed dirt.

The idiot appeared to be unharmed as well, only dazed. He was assisted away by family members.

She looked back toward Edwin Sorrels. "Thank you," she said through dry lips, and he acknowledged her words with an inclination of his head. "Are you certain you are not injured?" she asked.

"Quite certain."

Wishing to deny the curious any further reason to stay, she continued, "You must come back to the house, Mr. Sorrels, and I will look at your wounds."

He followed her out of the murmuring crowd and back toward the house.

"I have some skill with herbs and medicines," she said matter-of-factly as they walked toward the house. They made a curious pair, she realized, as people who had not attended the race turned to stare at them. She was all proper in her widow's weeds while his clothes were dirty and disheveled.

"I would like to examine you to make certain you are uninjured," she continued.

"That won't be necessary. I am fine."

"There's blood on your arm."

"A scratch. I'll see to it myself."

She did not argue further, for she sensed it would be pointless. Another thought occurred to her: there was no question now of asking him to leave. He had just saved a man's life, and she owed him a debt of gratitude.

They reached the house and stepped inside. Its thick walls kept the interior cool even on warm days. At the moment it felt very pleasant to be in out of the sun. They walked to the foot of the stairs and stopped.

Aware of the debt of gratitude she owed him, Cornelia cleared her throat and began formally, "I wish to express my sincere appreciation for your—"

"You needn't read me a speech." A grin cut his stern features. "You have already had to give one of those this week."

She blushed at the reminder of her halting welcoming speech yesterday morning.

"Don't color so. I'm only teasing you." In a gentler voice, he continued, "As a matter of fact, you have my sympathy. It must be difficult to try to fill your husband's shoes."

"I do not find it an onerous task," she said firmly. "I was fortunate enough to be married to an exceptionally fine man. It gives me pleasure to carry on in a way that would make him proud."

He watched her in guarded silence.

She colored under his gaze. Had she sounded overly dutiful to read Frederick's praises so loudly? But those were her true feelings for him.

"I must go upstairs and change into something more acceptable." Edwin Sorrels turned and mounted the stairs.

Even in his tattered clothes, he carried himself with a certain pride, she noted, and revised her opinion of him yet again. Perhaps he had been a soldier. How could she have thought him a simple country squire? And yet there was his poorly tutored accent. So many things about this man contradicted one other. One thing was certain, however; he was brave.

She resolutely put thoughts of him from her mind as she turned her attention to consulting with the temperamental chef over the evening's meal.

Later that afternoon Cornelia went outside to visit the fair. The sun was high in the sky, and the stalls were doing a brisk activity. She stopped at a booth selling lacquered boxes and smiled at one of her houseguests.

"Are you finding a box to take back as a gift, Lady Chapman?"

"Little need for that," the other woman replied, "since the whole of Plymouth seems to be here to buy their own boxes. No doubt they've come to learn the very latest on-dits."

Cornelia's smile deepened. "It seems passing strange for residents of Plymouth to come *here* to learn anything when the British fleet puts in there with all the latest news of how the war goes."

"Ah, yes, the war," Lady Chapman said with a

world-weary sigh. "Keeping the French prisoners there is bad enough without having to listen to military tales every time one goes to a dinner party. I came here to learn the *real* news—like what ladies will be wearing this Season in London."

Cornelia was not deceived. Everyone in the country awaited news of the war with anxious heart. If there was an invasion from across the Channel, it would be impossible to feel safe here in Devon. The coast was not so far away, after all.

When Frederick was alive, Cornelia had tried on several occasions to discuss the war with him, but he had always cut her off. "You have enough on your mind with seeing to a child and a household," he had told her shortly. "I am persuaded our shores are well defended, and you need not concern yourself about them." He had been willing to talk with her about almost every subject except Napoleon's France.

"That man standing by the silver booth was lately in Plymouth," Lady Chapman noted. "I am not acquainted with him, but I know he is one of your houseguests. Who is he, pray?"

Cornelia looked at the man two booths away and saw Edwin Sorrels. She frowned. Odd that he had been in Plymouth recently. He told her he had ridden in directly from London.

"He acted very bravely this morning," Lady Chapman noted mildly before moving on to the next booth to examine some fans.

"Yes," Cornelia murmured. He had acted with bravery, and she was grateful for that. But she still wondered how he had come into possession of her miniature. She could not ask him to leave now, but he would certainly leave of his own accord shortly.

After all, he had come to see Frederick. Since that was impossible, why should he remain? Cornelia still thought there was much about his visit that he had not told her. She also doubted she would ever have the opportunity to question her mysterious guest closely enough to learn the truth of his connection with Frederick.

Chapter 3

The day after the event at the racetrack Cornelia laid the sleeping baby back into the crib, smiled at the nanny, and tiptoed from the room. It was the middle of the afternoon, and the fair had slowed to a drowsy pace. Some of the booths had even closed, so the owners could rest before the evening activities began. Most of the guests had taken to their rooms for naps.

That left Cornelia with time to herself. She walked purposefully into her sitting room and paused to listen for sounds from the adjoining room where Edwin Sorrels was staying. Hearing none, she quietly opened the drawer of a large writing desk and removed a key. She carried the key into her bedroom, took a small wooden box from the bottom drawer of a highboy, and unlocked it.

Inside, tied with a red ribbon, lay the letters she and Frederick had written to each other when they were courting. Seeing the letters brought a mist to her eyes. Blinking away the wetness, she looked below the letters to the bundle of papers and documents. These had been atop her husband's desk when he died. A few days after his death, she had scooped everything off his desk and locked it all away. She had not yet had the fortitude to sort through the contents.

Now she was prompted to do so. All day long she had thought about why Edwin Sorrels had slipped into the sitting room two nights ago. He said he had been looking for something Frederick was keeping for him. She did not believe that, but he had certainly been searching for *something*. What?

Sitting on the edge of the bed, she smoothed her black muslin skirts, took a deep breath, and began looking at the papers. Most of them were letters from friends, bills from the tailor, or papers concerning the estate. She found nothing of sufficient interest to prompt someone to go prowling in the middle of the night.

Cornelia was almost to the bottom of the stack when she uncovered a small slip of paper that had obviously been torn from a larger page. On the paper was a cryptic message in her husband's handwriting. "Dirk, E.S. is in Paris. Needs list. I'll help. Fair." It was dated three days before Frederick's death.

Dazed, Cornelia turned the torn paper over. The back was blank. She had no idea who Dirk was. And she knew nothing of a list. E.S. . . . Was that Edwin Sorrels?

Cornelia continued to sit motionless. The slight churning in her stomach turned into an ache. Until this moment, she had believed with all her heart that she and Frederick had shared everything. Clearly that was not true. Something had been going on in his life that she had not been a part of. The knowledge that he had kept secrets from her cut deeply.

She rose numbly and put the box away. Her color was pale and her steps irresolute. What she really wanted to do was crawl beneath the covers and cry until she fell asleep, but she had a houseful of company to attend to and a fair to oversee. For the moment, she must bear up. Once the crowds were gone, she would be able to give in to this new grief in her life.

Lady Devenish looked taut and grim today, Edwin noted as he watched her examining copper bracelets in a booth near the corner of the fair. It was late afternoon and her companions, several females of about her age, kept glancing apprehensively up at the sky. Cornelia seemed not to notice the threatening weather.

What had been a breeze a few hours earlier was bidding fair to becoming a gale. Dark clouds covered the sky. From the distance came the unmistakable roll of thunder. In the stalls that had walls and roofs, merchants continued business, but in the trestle booths which had no overhead covering, children and wives hastened to cover the wares with rough woolen blankets. Traders who operated only from a cart were busy shoving merchandise back into wooden boxes.

In the Great Booth, the dwarfs continued the play *As You Like It*, but the audience seated on the grass was only half attending. People kept looking worriedly toward the sky.

Finally a few large drops of rain fell. Edwin saw Cornelia look up in surprise. Then she spied him. Turning, she said a few words to her companions before she marched over to him.

The purposefulness of her stride and the firm set

of her jaw told him all he needed to know about her mood. He feared she would ask him how he had gotten into the sitting room the other night. Locked doors were of little consequence to him, but he could scarcely tell her that. He was not sure what he would say if confronted.

As it happened, however, that was not her question.

She drew to a stiff halt in front of him and said tersely, "I wish a word with you, Mr. Sorrels. About my husband," she added deliberately.

It was not a conversation he wished to have, but he saw no choice. "As you wish, but I fancy we shall shortly be wet if we try to talk here."

Cornelia was not to be put off. "We will go somewhere out of the rain."

Edwin expected her to lead the way into the house. Instead she started around the side of the ancient manor house. He followed. The flowing quality to her walk drew his eyes to her hips. She was a solid, nicely shaped woman, he noted. He had never cared for wispy little creatures. His preference was for women like Cornelia with graceful stature and strong, womanly curves. Suddenly aware that the lady he was watching was wearing widow's black, Edwin looked away.

As thunder rolled again and rain began to fall in earnest, Cornelia entered a gate and led him into a garden aromatic with the scent of herbs. She continued into a gardener's shed. There she stopped and turned to face him. "We can talk freely here," she said. Her hair was damp with the rain and her gown was speckled with drops, but she seemed not to care.

"Lady Devenish, I apologize again for my intrusion the other night. It was unforgiveable and—"

She cut him off. "What was Frederick doing when he died?"

Her question took him unaware. "I was given to understand he was in a carriage on his way back from visiting a friend," he said carefully

"I don't mean that." Her voice was querulous, and he realized she was close to tears. To fend them off, she kept her head tilted up at a regal angle.

"I do not know what he was doing," he said quietly.

"But you *do* know that he was involved in things about which I knew nothing." Her words were an accusation, and her dark eyes were bright with unshed tears.

No longer able to hold her gaze, he looked away. She was asking for answers. As Frederick's widow, she had a right to them. But he could not reply without jeopardizing others.

She blinked resolutely against the tears. "Mr. Sorrels, I would remind you that we are at war with France. We have been off and on since 1803, as well you know. Those who go to Paris do so at considerable risk, and yet I have discovered papers indicating you were there. One would have to have a very important reason to venture there." She looked him squarely in the eye.

If she knew he had been in Paris, she had indeed discovered papers of importance. Had she found the information he needed?

He cleared his throat and began cautiously, "Lady Devenish, I ask your help. Frederick was a loyal citizen who tried to help his king. More than that I cannot say, but I beg that you would keep this knowledge about Paris to yourself."

Her face was aglow with color. Hot pink stained her cheeks, and her eyes were a dark smokey brown. "How can you have the audacity to ask for my silence when you have given me no information?" she demanded angrily.

He didn't know whether to be touched by the pain in her eyes or steeled by the challenge in her voice. "There is nothing to say beyond what I have told you. If you have discovered any information, it is important that you give it to me."

"I have no intention of sharing anything with you," she said coldly. "I want answers; I am not here to respond to your questions. Was Frederick killed because of this involvement?"

"I don't know."

"You *do* know but you choose not to tell me. What part do you play in all of this?"

"I was an acquaintance of Frederick's."

"That tells me nothing. He had many acquaintances, but none of them were searching his desk after his death."

"I have given you all the information I can."

They were at an impasse, and they both knew it. For the space of a few seconds her flinty brown eyes met his remote green eyes. Then she turned on her heel and swept away.

Edwin watched her go. She had more spirit than he had credited her with. Did she know anything of importance? Probably not, he decided. If she had found the list of names, she would have questioned him about them as well as about Paris.

There was little doubt in his mind she wanted

him to leave. But he would not do so yet. He still had not found what he had come for.

The banquet was held in true medieval style, the way it had been held when the fair began in the 1500s.

Tonight was Midsummer Eve, a time of magic. It was the night when fairies and witches were rumored to be abroad. It was the night to gather the mystical fern seed which had the power to make its wearer invisible and to guide the bearer to hidden treasure.

In a tradition that stretched back beyond anyone's memory, fires were lit on the tops of the hills surrounding the fairground. Looking through the windows of the great hall, Cornelia saw the fires glowing red and golden. Inside the hall was a Midsummer candle circle. Tiny flames danced upon the tallow candles.

Cornelia sat at the high table on the dais with the most distinguished guests. The majority of those present were relatives of Frederick. The dowager sat beside Cornelia. The Surveyor of Ceremonies had just presented the salt to the guests at the high table, and now he waved his key to summon the Pantler to cut the bread.

In the past, Cornelia had enjoyed the solemn pomp and circumstance of the occasion, which was so in contrast to the loud merriment taking place in the yard outside. This evening, however, it was impossible to enjoy anything. Knowing that Frederick had kept secrets from her saddened and disturbed her.

Her gaze traveled to where Edwin Sorrels sat at a trestle table not far from hers. He looked restless and uncomfortable, as if he were little accustomed to affairs such as this. She was certain he had spent scant time in society. What *had* he done with his time, and how had that involved Frederick?

Cornelia was intelligent, but she knew that matching wits with her guest would be no easy task. She wanted to dislike him, but she admitted to a grudging admiration. He had been brave in rescuing that poor idiot. Even when she had confronted him in the middle of the night in the sitting room, he had been at pains to reassure her and keep her from being frightened.

Cornelia straightened abruptly, annoyed with herself for showing any tolerance for the man.

He had asked her not to tell anyone what she had learned from Frederick's note, but Cornelia had made no such promise. She owed him nothing. Before looking at Frederick's papers this afternoon, she would have said her duty was to her husband's memory. She was no longer certain of that. Clearly Frederick had been involved with some type of spying. The only thing she did not know was whether he had been loyal to the Crown or a traitor to England.

The possibility that her husband might have been disloyal to the Crown was more than she could bear. Even if Frederick had been loyal, that did not mean that Edwin Sorrels was.

Cornelia brought her attention back to the high table where the bishop waxed eloquent over the blessing of the Wassail. He finally concluded and the horns, trumpets, and bells signaled the beginning of the first of twenty-nine courses.

Twenty-nine courses. This would take hours. She thought of little Elizabeth asleep upstairs in her cradle and endured because of her. Whatever doubts Cornelia might harbor toward Frederick, Elizabeth was still his daughter. The title had gone to a male heir, but this property had not gone with the title. The tiny girl was heiress to the estate and all the traditions that surrounded it. Cornelia believed that her duty as a mother was to preserve the estate's traditions even if her faith in Frederick was shaken.

Beside her the dowager conversed with Alan, one of the North Country Devenishes. He was a pleasant man whose hair had thinned on top until he had only a few fine hairs left, with which he tried valiantly to conceal a bald dome.

"It's absurd to send your oldest girl to London to find a husband," the dowager pronounced tartly. "Why, look at Cornelia. She never went to London and she made a splendid match. In fact, she was fortunate enough to marry above her station."

Cornelia stifled a sigh.

"My daughter wishes to see more of the world," Alan said. "I've promised her a Season."

"Such foolishness. Few of the Devenishes go to London, so she won't even be among family there. I'll wager she'll do nothing but cost you money. The Devenishes are a good, old family, but we are not of the highest nobility," the old woman said bluntly. "In London she may find herself possessing little to attract a man. Cornelia would have a difficult time finding someone should she wish to remarry. I am persuaded she will spend the rest of her days alone."

Her mother-in-law spoke loudly enough to be heard down the table. Her prediction that Cornelia would remain unwed was met with surprised and sympathetic glances. On Cornelia's other side, Hortense patted her hand sympathetically and leaned over to whisper, "Pay her no mind."

But that was difficult when a blush of pure embarrassment was creeping up her neck. The dowager had been easier to endure when Frederick was alive. Now, in her grief, she seemed driven to spread the pain she felt.

Looking up again, Cornelia noted with embarrassed horror that Edwin Sorrels had heard the exchange. He was studying her speculatively, as if measuring for himself her chances of finding another husband. Flushing crimson, she looked away.

"Cornelia is a handsome woman," Alan said gallantly. "I should be surprised if she did not attract some man's notice as soon as she is out of mourning."

The old woman shrugged. "Perhaps."

"None as worthy as Frederick," he added diplomatically.

The courses continued.

Cornelia was careful not to look in Edwin Sorrel's direction for the remainder of the evening. It annoyed her that she was so aware of his presence. He should have had the grace to take his leave after their conversation in the gardener's shed this afternoon. Yet he remained.

The feast continued until after midnight. Even though Cornelia was not sleepy, she was glad to see the guests finally depart for their rooms.

With the Midsummer moon hanging like a gleaming lantern in the sky, she was lured outdoors. She did not intend to go far, and there was still enough activity around the fire pyres for her to feel safe out alone.

She walked to the herb garden, pausing to inhale its wondrous scents. She and Frederick had sometimes come here in the evenings and sat on the stone wall together holding hands. The memory saddened her. It also unleashed a brooding anger. What had Frederick really been thinking when they were here together? Had he thought about her or about his meetings with Dirk and heaven only knew who else?

She was turning back toward the house when she saw the faint glimmer of a light far in the woods. Who would have a lantern in such a remote place? The gypsies? Curious, she ventured into the woods.

The air felt cooler beneath the trees, and the ground was spongy from the recent rain. It was hardly the sort of night for anyone to be in the woods—certainly not gypsies. They usually had large fires in the open and wild music with a woman in brightly colored skirts spinning and leaping around the blaze.

As curiosity pulled her further into the woods, Cornelia realized this was a quiet group. It was not a fire at all, she realized, but a lantern that was partially covered, as if those gathered meant to conceal it from being seen. Who would feel it necessary to meet in such secrecy?

She stopped when she was close enough to distinguish faces. Only three people were gathered. The trio included a gypsy woman whom Cornelia had seen reading palms and a dwarf. The third person was hidden in shadows. From this distance it looked almost like the local vicar, but, of course, it could not be.

They were using the lantern to illuminate a paper or a map that they were peering over. They spoke to each other in voices so low Cornelia could not hear them.

Then they folded the paper and began to rise. Cornelia lifted her skirts and hurried back toward the house.

Lying in bed half an hour later, her curiosity was still aroused. But the fair was a time of strange things, she reminded herself. Midsummer night brought out an eerie, gothic restlessness in people. If some of those people had taken to the woods for further conversation, it would not be the strangest thing that had ever happened at the fair.

"What can you tell me about that night?" Edwin asked the nervous-looking boy named Jack. He had been with Lord Devenish the night he was killed.

"It was dark," Jack mumbled, kicking at the hard-packed dirt on the stable floor. "I didn't see much. A man stopped the coach and opened the door and shot Sir Frederick. That's all I know." He looked up anxiously. "Are you done w' me then?"

"No."

The two were in the back room of the stables. Bridles and harnesses hung from nails on the walls around them. The tack room smelled of old leather and fresh straw. The sound of horses pawing the floor came from nearby.

"Did the intruder speak at all?" Edwin asked.

"No."

"Was he tall?"

"I couldn't tell. He was bent over in the doorway. I was too scared to notice much."

"I daresay that's true." Edwin let a moment pass in silence. "How long have you worked here, Jack?"

"Since I was twelve. I'm fourteen now," he added.

"Do you like it here?"

"Yes sir. Lady Devenish makes sure everyone gets treated fine." The ghost of a smile crossed his face. "She makes sure we eat well, too."

Edwin's purpose was to find out what had happened the night Sir Frederick was killed. But since the boy had brought up Lady Devenish's name, Edwin pursued the matter. "You like your mistress, Jack?"

"Yes, sir. She took care of me once when I had the fever. She has soft hands," he added reverently.

"I see."

"She's as fine an 'erbalist as ever you'll see," Jack volunteered. "I've helped her gather hawthorn flowers. She uses 'em to draw thorns and blisters from the skin, and she can cure bruises with purple iris petals and—" He stopped, reddening at having said so much. "She's cured a number of the villagers," he mumbled in closing.

The boy was infatuated with Lady Devenish, Edwin realized. Such an attraction was natural enough. After all, Cornelia was a handsome woman, and she had obviously been gentle with Jack.

Edwin almost regretted that she disliked him so much. He wouldn't mind having someone with soft hands and big brown eyes be gentle with him now and again. There had been some hellish moments in France when the thought of a woman back in

44

England worrying about him and anxious to nurture him might have made the torment easier to bear.

He pushed aside such futile thoughts. He had escaped from France, and all that was in the past. In a few days he would be gone from here. If Cornelia did not like him, there were plenty of other women who would certainly welcome his attention.

"Are you done with me, sir?" the boy asked again.

"For the moment. Tonight, though, I would like you to ride with me and show me the spot where Sir Frederick was killed."

"After dark?" The boy looked fearful.

"Yes." He smiled fleetingly. "I have a large gun, Jack, and I know how to use it. You need not worry about anyone setting on us this time."

"Aye." But he still looked doubtful.

Edwin filled the boy's palm with enough coins to change his expression to one of delight. "There's more for you if you tell no one of our talk or of our ride."

"Right enough, sir." Jack left the saddle room reverently pocketing his newfound wealth.

Edwin sighed. He wished all his problems could be solved so easily. Natale had reported back that she had learned nothing so far, and he had found out disappointingly little from Jack. Still, seeing where the shooting actually happened might give him some ideas. It was a slim hope but all he had at the moment.

He had crept back into Lady Devenish's room today while she was out and had found the note concerning E.S. and Paris as well as some other

papers. None of them had been the priceless paper listing those highly placed people in London who were involved in spying. He was beginning to fear that that knowledge had died with Frederick.

Chapter 4

The Mumming Play about Robin Hood ended, and several performers jumped down from the stage.

"Now we're going to let *you* entertain us," one of the dwarfs announced.

The actors began pulling people from the audience and coaxing them onto the stage. A farrier's daughter with blond hair and a shining smile was urged up onto the stage by two dwarfs. A stocky tradesman was recruited and went along laughing to the center of the stage. Two of Cornelia's houseguests were selected from beside her.

"Now we need a lover for the beauteous maiden," one of the dwarfs proclaimed and scanned the audience critically.

On the stage the farrier's daughter blushed prettily.

"How about you, my good man?"

Cornelia saw a performer tap Edwin Sorrels on the shoulder. "Don't be bashful. Come along."

"I don't really—"

"You may get a chance to kiss the pretty maid," the actor offered as enticement.

At that several men in the audience raised their

hands to volunteer, while others shouted catcalls and general male encouragement.

Edwin went.

Cornelia watched. Edwin Sorrels did look the part of a romantic lead, she acknowledged grudgingly. With his dark good looks, he could have played that part on any stage. The fact she knew him to be a man of mystery lent an additional edge to the role.

Edwin listened attentively as one of the dwarfs whispered his lines to him. Across the stage, the pretty girl was being coached by a female performer.

Then the players were ready to take their places. The drama, helped along by the regular actors, was a hammy romance played for laughs.

The girl was supposed to be a shopkeeper's daughter named Eshrieka, and Edwin played a king. He has come to Eshrieka's village looking for the dragon that had stolen the golden unicorn. She knew where the dragon lived, but before she could tell him, Edwin had to prove he was a king by bringing back three "gifts." The first gift she demanded was a robin's feather.

"Where shall I find a robin's feather?" the "king" mused in a loud stage voice.

"That bloke at the edge of the stage is holding one," someone on the front row offered helpfully.

Indeed one of the dwarfs was standing gamely at the edge of the stage holding a feather.

Edwin bypassed that. To Cornelia's surprise and the delight of the audience, he went instead to a lady in the third row and plucked a feather from her bonnet. He returned to the stage and presented the billowing feather to Eshrieka with the most exaggerated of courtly bows Cornelia had ever seen.

"Really, the man is a shameless ham," Cornelia told Hortense as Edwin turned and grinned at the audience.

Eshrieka smiled shyly, batted her eyelashes, and sent him off to find a gem.

The dwarf stood at the edge of the stage helpfully holding a ridiculously large glittering bauble that was meant to be a diamond.

But the king went back out into the audience and coaxed a diamond pin from a flustered, delighted matron. He leaped back up onto the stage and delivered the gem to the maiden with a flourish.

The audience burst into spontaneous applause.

As his final trial, the maiden sent him off to find an honest man.

The whole play revolved around Edwin Sorrels, Cornelia was forced to admit. He had a playful charisma that was lacking in the others on the stage. She had not suspected him of possessing such a spirit of fun. Having experienced little fun since Frederick's death, Cornelia found that quality very appealing.

Catching the drift of her own thoughts, she straightened sternly. The man might be engaging, but he was also a rogue. At the very least he had taken part in some highly suspicious activities in her home. She was not going to allow herself to be captivated by him.

The audience had no such reservations. They loved Edwin.

He searched the audience diligently, going row by row and pausing now and then looking for an honest man. He returned to the stage and announced woefully. "My lovely Eshrieka, after a long and arduous search I have determined the only honest man on the earth is myself."

The audience laughed and clapped thunderously.

"You have won the fair lady," one of the regular actors said. "You may now kiss her."

The young woman looked becomingly confused. She blushed a lovely shade of rose as Edwin advanced purposefully toward her.

"Give 'er a good 'un!" a rough voice behind Cornelia shouted.

Several men in the audience stamped their feet. A woman somewhere murmured, "Lucky child."

Edwin bent toward Eshrieka.

Cornelia looked away.

Beneath the dark canopy of the trees the night felt cool. Edwin galloped down the deserted road. Jack rode ahead on a smaller horse. Every now and again the boy glanced nervously back to reassure himself that Edwin was still behind him.

As the pair entered the shadow of the trees, Jack turned around again. His voice was a rough whisper on the night wind. "Here, sir, this is where it happened. Just in this bend."

Edwin pulled his horse to a halt and dismounted. Jack reluctantly stopped and slid down.

Ignoring him, Edwin looked up toward the half moon. Was this what the sky had looked like the night Frederick had been killed? Was this how the air had felt? Had Frederick had any inkling of what was to come?

The road was deserted, just as it had been that night. Except for the heavy breathing of the horses, all was silence.

A man lying in wait could have hidden behind any of the trees.

"You are certain you didn't hear a horse, Jack?"

"No, sir."

Edwin glanced back toward the wood. The murderer must have tied his horse some distance away. Otherwise, the coach horses could have picked up the scent and have given some sign of nervousness. Ambushes on deserted stretches were common enough, but this was nothing more than a farmer's road into a small town. No rich nobles were likely to ride this way.

An ordinary highwayman would have to be stupid to set up station here and lie in wait. That meant the man who had ambushed Frederick had known exactly who he was waiting for and what time Frederick would pass. That also indicated the killer was someone who lived in the area. Probably it had been someone who had seen Frederick in the village and knew he would be driving this lonely stretch of road on his way back home.

"Where were you returning from, Jack?"

"The squire's," he replied impatiently.

He had already told Edwin as much. The squire, an elderly, gout-ridden man, seemed innocent enough. That did not mean, however, that it could not have been someone from his household.

"Did you notice any of the servants watching you as you left the squire's house?"

"No, sir. Please, can we go now, sir?" Jack asked nervously.

Edwin nodded. There was nothing more to be gained from staying. He had seen what he had come to see. Besides, he was to meet Natale in the forest in a short time. Remounting his bay, he headed back toward the house.

As the pair rode without speaking, Edwin's thoughts remained on Frederick. He thought of the last time he saw Frederick. It had been ten months ago. He and Frederick had been at Calais searching in the darkness for the boat that was to take them back to England.

"Where in the devil did they hide the damned thing?" Edwin had muttered. They talked in low voices and crouched low as they walked. Patrols were heavy along this stretch of the French coast. However, since one had passed only a few minutes ago, they felt relatively safe. Still, an edge of caution remained. Both knew if they were caught, they would be shot on sight.

"Linton said it would be south of the stone church. It's got to be here." After a moment's silence, he said, "Cornelia will be angry with me when I return. I told her I would be gone a week seeing to lands I own in Cornwall. I have been away three weeks already, and it'll be another week before I get home."

"Buy her a pretty bauble," Edwin suggested without interest. Where was the damned boat?

Frederick laughed shortly. "A lot you know about wives. They're not like lightskirts. Wives will take the pretty trinkets and still ask questions."

"You seem happy though," Edwin noted disinterestedly as he peered through the half light of the moon along the coast looking among the rushes for the boat.

"I am. Cornelia is a good woman."

"You are lucky." Edwin didn't mean a word of

it. He could conceive of nothing more boring than being legshackled to a "good woman."

"I have her likeness with me. Have I ever shown it to you?"

"No."

"Here."

Edwin took the miniature Frederick shoved toward him and glanced at it. In the moonlight, he could tell little about the woman in the picture. "She's handsome," he said perfunctorily. Just then he caught sight of the boat sticking through the grass at the edge of the water and breathed a sigh of relief.

He and Frederick both heard the horses' hooves at the same time.

"Bloody hell! Let's get out of here."

Edwin jammed the locket into his pocket and ran for the boat. He pushed off and jumped in. Frederick was already rowing furiously by the time the bullets began whizzing over their heads.

Grabbing the second pair of oars, Edwin rowed, too.

He and Frederick had laughed about those moments afterward. But not until they were safe in Dover and filled with enough glasses of stout to make the bullets seem less frightening.

That was the last time Edwin had seen Frederick. He had forgotten the locket until his valet produced it a few days later.

Jack's voice brought Edwin back to the present. "Will you be needin' me again then?"

Glancing up, he saw they were back at the stables. "No." He reached into his pockets and found more coins for Jack. "See to my horse."

He left his bay at the stable, sauntered through

the fair and melted into the woods and down a narrow path.

He and Jack had stayed out longer than he had expected. He hoped Natale was not waiting for him. Was that her behind him? He turned but saw only darkness. Strange, he thought he had heard something.

He had scarcely turned back before he felt a heavy hand on his neck and suffered a numbing blow to his head. He fell forward and was unconscious before the second blow struck him.

Little Elizabeth felt warm and soft as Cornelia picked her up that night from her cradle. Sitting in a low chair beside the cradle, she loosened her chemise and let the baby breast-feed.

For the first time today Cornelia felt satisfied. She didn't take her eyes off her daughter. She had so little time to spend with this most precious of all her duties that she did not want to miss a minute of it.

As the baby nursed, Cornelia murmured, "Is my darling baby hungry?" She touched Elizabeth's wispy hair.

Cornelia had never imagined herself as one who would talk nonsense to her child. She had been surprised to discover a number of things about herself when she became a mother. One was the fierce protectiveness she felt toward tiny Elizabeth. Another was the softness that motherhood had brought out in her.

Before Elizabeth's birth, Frederick had teased her that having a child would mellow her toward the whole world. That had not happened. Frederick's death and the fact she was suddenly thrust at the head of the household had forced Cornelia to be strong. Only in her private moments with Elizabeth did Cornelia allow herself to show the true softness of which she was capable.

In the face of these new facts about Frederick, she realized she was going to have to be even stronger. Regret and anger surfaced. How could the man she had trusted have deceived her so? And why? What had he been embroiled in at the time of his death?

The baby, sensing her mother's agitation, began to squirm and cry.

"There, there."

Cornelia cradled the child closer against her bare skin and willed herself to be calm again. But the anger was still there, and she knew it. Rising, she placed Elizabeth back in her cradle. She would wait to hold her child when she felt more at peace with the world.

Right now sleep was the best medicine.

Cornelia bent and placed a kiss on her baby's pink forehead, started from the room, and then returned for just one more parting kiss. She blew out all except one of the candles and went to her own room.

The day had been eventful. Once she was in bed she did not immediately fall asleep. Instead she lay in the darkness and analyzed things. She thought about a tense conversation she had had with the dowager and about her moments with Elizabeth. But mostly she thought about Edwin Sorrels.

Lying in the soft, sensual cocoon of her cotton bedclothes, she recalled Edwin's engaging smile as he stood on the stage. She thought about the contours of his legs in his dun-colored breeches, and she thought about the strong shape of his back as he had bent toward the flustered Eshrieka to kiss her.

Alone in the confines of her room, Cornelia did what no woman, least of all a widow should do—she imagined him kissing her. She imagined those bold lips settling atop hers with purpose and passion, and she almost felt his strong arms encircling her and drawing her closer to him.

Cornelia sat bolt upright in bed, flushed with the guilt of her totally unacceptable passion. How could she—a mother, a widow, and a lady—permit her thoughts to be such toward Edwin Sorrels? It was a sign of how truly alone she felt that she would be attracted to a completely inappropriate man.

Even after she laid back in the bed, it was several moments before her pulse returned to normal and her body became again that of a modest woman. Finally she fell asleep.

Cornelia was lost in a dreamless sleep when something pulled her back toward waking. Murmuring a garbled protest, she turned over and tried to sink back into her slumber.

But something kept pulling her toward the surface. There it was again. Someone was shaking her and urging her to wake up.

"What?" she asked groggily.

"You must get up. Quickly!"

It was a woman, Cornelia realized. Fully awake now, she blinked at the blond-haired woman standing over her holding a candle. She recognized the intruder as Natale, the woman who performed magic.

Cornelia sat up in the bed. "What are you doing here?"

"There's been an accident. Come quickly. Bring your herbs and medicines."

That was all the explanation Cornelia needed. She had been roused more than once in the middle of the night for an emergency. She threw back the covers. She dressed quickly in a sturdy gray walking dress, grabbed a heavy pelisse from her wardrobe and slipped on a pair of shoes. Then she picked up the black bag she always kept in her room. All the while Natale stood by the door urging her to hurry.

"I'm ready." Cornelia rushed out the door after the fey-looking blond woman. They hurried down the hall, guided only by the flickering light of Natale's candle.

She stepped outside and felt the full force of the night coolness through the thin soles of her shoes. Ignoring her discomfort, she pulled her pelisse closer around her shoulders and started toward the sleeping quarters of the performers.

Natale grabbed her arm. "Not there. This way."

The candle lasted only a moment in the crisp air. Thankfully the half moon provided enough light to illuminate the roots of trees as they rushed toward the forest. The heavy bag Cornelia carried banged against her legs as she ran after Natale. She was too breathless to ask where they were going. They plunged further into the forest. Cornelia's heart was pounding from exertion before Natale finally stopped near the pond.

"Here," Natale said urgently. She relit the candle and held it up, sheltering its flame with one hand.

Cornelia knelt in the cold, wet grass. A man lay on his side, motionless. A nasty gash on the back

57

of his head indicated he had been hit from behind. She looked closer and saw that the man was Edwin Sorrels.

"What happened?"

"It doesn't matter. You must help him."

Cornelia looked back at the cut. She was used to dealing with farm injuries and fevers and cuts that had festered, but she had never treated a head wound before. "He needs a doctor."

"No! No one else must know."

Cornelia looked up into Natale's sharply intense face and knew there was no changing her mind.

"I'll do what I can," she said grimly. "Hold the candle closer."

Cornelia began to clean the wound. She was surprised at how anxious she felt as she went about her work. Normally she was cool and in control when applying balms and poultices, but now her hands shook slightly.

As Cornelia worked, Natale looked around anxiously.

Edwin groaned.

"It's all right," Cornelia whispered comfortingly. He was unconscious, but she saw the pain etched in the handsome lines of his face. Impulsively she stroked his forehead, as if by doing so, she could smooth out the lines of pain. Touching his chilled brow brought feelings of protectiveness and tenderness to the surface.

"You'll be fine," she murmured, her voice a soothing lilt as she worked at cleaning the wound and bandaging it.

Cornelia could tell he had lain here awhile for in places the blood had clotted into a dark mat. His skin felt cool to the touch, and she worried what the exposure to the night air would do to him. Even as that thought went through her mind, Natale pulled off her heavy wool shawl and laid it over Edwin. It was not enough, but it would help until they could get him out of here.

Cornelia kept her touch gentle and continued to comfort him with a litany of soft words.

Finally, she had the wound bandaged to her satisfaction. Rising, she slipped off her petticoat. Then she knelt down again. With as much care as if she were tending Elizabeth, she lifted his head and placed the petticoat as a pillow.

She looked up at Natale. "We must get him in out of the cold."

"I'll take care of that."

"Some men from the house can—"

"I'll see to it," Natale said brusquely. "Can you find your way back to the house?"

"Yes, of course, but—"

"Go quickly."

Cornelia looked worriedly down at the injured man. She thought of how vital and full of life he had looked earlier today. Now his skin was pale and his breathing shallow. "I can't go off and leave him like this."

"You must. Every moment you stay endangers him more." Natale rose. "You must not tell anyone about this." She peered into Cornelia's face. "Do you understand?"

Amazingly, a part of her did understand. Natale's desperation transmitted itself to Cornelia. Clearly someone who meant Edwin harm had done this to him. The thought of Frederick's death flashed through her mind, and she knew Edwin's injury and Frederick's death were somehow connected. With a terse nod, Cornelia turned and made her way back to the house.

As she hurried through the night woods, she was afraid. She feared for Edwin and Natale and herself. Whoever had done this to Edwin might still be lurking in the forest.

She tensed at every night bird's call and sucked in a frightened breath when something darted in front of her. It was only a squirrel, she realized, but her heart was still thumping hard.

She breathed a sigh of relief once she reached the house, but it was not until she was back in her own bed with the door locked behind her that she felt truly safe.

Sleep was impossible. She lay in the big, empty bed fretting about the seriousness of Edwin's injury. He had been hit with vicious force. The wound was deep. She had seen enough injuries to know that things could go wrong in healing, and that made her doubly worried. If only they could have called a doctor.

Early the next morning Cornelia was still awake. She dressed without calling her maid. After going upstairs and nursing the baby, she donned the same pelisse she had worn last night, left the house, and retraced her steps.

When she reached the spot where Edwin had lain, she found only matted grass and a few rust-colored stains that must have been blood.

Anxious for word of Edwin, she sought out Natale's tent in the area where the performers were staying. The tent was gone. A sleepy dwarf sipping coffee outside his own tent informed her Natale had departed some time in the night.

"Did anyone see her go?" Cornelia demanded.

He shrugged and rubbed his eyes. "I didn't. You might ask some of the others when they get up."

She nodded.

Although she returned to the performer's living area twice that day, she did not locate anyone who knew anything. Her concern for Edwin slowly began to turn to anger. The least Natale could have done was say good-bye and send her word of Edwin's condition.

Cornelia had too much on her mind to dwell on her bitterness long. This was the last day of the fair and the day passed in a blur of activities. Final shows were given on the performing grounds. Last minute bargains were struck between merchants and those eager to buy their wares. The day ended with an elaborate ball.

Cornelia dressed for the ball in a black gown with a neckline cut high and demure. She glanced at herself in the cheval glass before going downstairs but was too distracted to notice the dress failed to conceal the rich swell of her bosom or that her narrow waist beckoned a man's hands.

She thought of herself as a widow and assumed that everyone else, men included, did too. She was doing her best to put aside the unwidowly thoughts she had had last night concerning Edwin Sorrels.

As soon as she entered the great hall, fluttery Lady Chapman approached her. "What has become of that charming Mr. Sorrels, Cornelia? Someone said he had gone."

"He was called away unexpectedly." Cornelia hoped her flush did not betray her lie.

"How dreadful. I had so hoped to see him again. I wanted to tell him how utterly charming he was in the play."

"He already knows," Cornelia said drily. Her resentment toward her erstwhile guest was escalating. What had he been doing in the middle of the forest before he was hit? She wished he had never come to the fair at all. It would have made her life much less complicated.

"You must give him my regards when you write to him," Lady Chapman said breezily.

"Indeed, I shall." Cornelia would not write to Edwin Sorrels even if she knew his direction. And he would certainly not be welcome here should he ever return.

Chapter 5

The next day the last guests departed, and Cornelia was alone again. A new dimension had been added to her solitude. Now that she was no longer busy with other things, she was forced to look at Frederick's betrayal. The shock of learning that he had led a life about which she knew nothing changed to a sense of betrayal over the next weeks and months.

As the fall slid into early winter, she had all too much time alone to ponder how she was to accept the fact her husband had withheld secrets from her. In her mind, she reviewed conversations they had had and looked for new meanings to them. She thought about the times he had said he was going to visit a neighbor or a friend and now she wondered what he had really been doing.

Even with the diversion of her beloved daughter, the days were long and lonely. Winter deepened and Cornelia sat inside the chilly house and tried to occupy herself with tatting and reading to Elizabeth. Frederick's mother grew steadily more critical and irritable, and Cornelia winced at the thought of spending more long months with her. But what else did her future hold?

It was a particularly dismal day in late winter when a simple black carriage rolled down the muddy lane. Cornelia watched as Margaret Simpson, the vicar's sister, alighted. Margaret was a sprightly woman in her late twenties who had never been married. She had always been politely cordial to Cornelia. Although the two were not close friends, Cornelia felt warm toward her because she had been particularly attentive at the time of Frederick's death. She had been one of the few people who had urged Cornelia to talk about her feelings and about Frederick. The vicar, like any good vicar, had encouraged her to come to talk to him of her grief should she have the need.

Cornelia pulled her wool shawl closer around her against the chill of the big house and greeted her visitor at the door. "Margaret, how very good to see you!" Cornelia's reception was all the warmer because the day was so dreary and overcast. It was a pleasure to see someone from outside the household.

"Dear Cornelia, you look so pale. Are you feeling quite the thing?"

She gave a small laugh as she led Margaret into a parlor off the great hall. A fire blazed in the grate. "Yes. I am only bored."

"It *is* dreadful to be locked up in a house all winter," Margaret commiserated. She took off her bonnet and brushed at her dark red curls. "How is little Elizabeth? I have brought her a toy."

"How thoughtful. She will love it."

Cornelia rang for tea. Then she settled into a brocade chair and prepared for a coze. She was not dis-

64

appointed. Margaret was full of news about the birth of the Amberson's twins and of the scandalous doings of old Mrs. Baxter's daughter who had gone on the stage.

"But enough of my chatter. What of yourself, Cornelia?" Margaret interrupted herself to ask. "What have you been doing these past weeks? I only see you at church, and then I have not been able to say more than a word or two to you."

"I don't do anything," Cornelia said with a touch of self-pity. "I am here alone much of the time."

"We must change that," Margaret said firmly. "As soon as spring comes, you must make a trip. No wonder you're pale. One would be from sitting about this dull house. You will be out of mourning in a matter of weeks. Once you are, you must do something gay. You should go somewhere different, talk to new people and see different sights."

The idea sounded appealing even if it was not something Cornelia intended to act upon. Still, there was nothing wrong with dreaming. "Where would I go?" she asked for sake of conversation.

"Bath, perhaps. Or Brighton. No, I know where. You must go to London," Margaret decided with a brisk nod of her head. "Have you ever been there?"

Cornelia shook her head.

"Then it is settled. London it is."

The thought did tug at her fancy. Could she really do such a thing? Doubts crept forward. "What of Elizabeth? I cannot go off and leave her even for a day."

"Take her, of course."

"But I can't go by myself." And the thought of traveling with Frederick's mother washed her enthusiasm for the trip away.

"You can find a companion," Margaret said.

"I don't know. . . . That isn't so easy to do." But the idea grew more enticing even as she protested.

"Then *I* shall go with you. Surely you cannot object to that. We can take a lovely house somewhere and enjoy all the entertainments of London."

"You would go with me?" This was a blessing too good to be true.

Margaret smiled confidentially. "I have been wanting to go for some time. Talking you into it suits my plans very well, Cornelia."

"Oh."

"What do you say? Shall we make plans? Don't bite at your lip and hesitate. You needn't worry that I would be constantly underfoot, and that we would tire of each other. I would see to my own amusement. But it would be perfectly respectable if the two of us lived together."

'Where would we stay?"

"I know a woman I can write to who can find us lodgings that would not be too dear. I know that money is not a troublesome issue for you, but I have not so much as you. But I have saved up for a long time and I believe I have enough. Will you go?"

Cornelia was done with hesitation. "Yes," she declared.

"Splendid."

It was amazing how much faster the bleak winter days passed now that Cornelia was busy planning her trip. She and Margaret consulted often. The vicar's sister came with guidebooks and the two of them had a wonderful time anticipating the journey. At Margaret's insistence, Cornelia perused fashion plates and ordered some dresses from a local seamstress.

Now that she was out of mourning, it was acceptable for her to wear brighter colors. But she stayed with subdued browns and quiet grays. Her hair had grown longer over the winter, and she had it styled into a decorous bun that she wore low on her neck. She knew the clothes and hairstyle made her look older than her years, but that did not matter. For what reason would she wish to look glamorous? It was more important that she look like a respectable widow.

Cornelia thought she was the picture of propriety the day she and Margaret arrived at the house they had taken in London. Not that she was paying much attention to herself. She was more preoccupied with inspecting the house.

The woman through whom Margaret had taken the house had written that it was in a genteel Mayfair neighborhood. It was not one of the grand houses in St. James Square but it was nicely proportioned in a Grecian style, even having four columns across the front. She had assured them that rows of windows on every side allowed for plenty of light. There was a beautiful walled-in garden in the back. The house had five bedrooms on the second floor and a small nursery on the third floor near the servants' sleeping rooms. It would be the perfect house for them, the woman had concluded.

Cornelia was inclined to agree as she followed Margaret inside the carved front door and looked around. The walls were a serene cream color and the ceiling mouldings exquisitely carved.

"It's lovely," she said.

"Yes," Margaret agreed.

While the servants carried in bandboxes and trunks and dumped them in the entryway to be sorted later, Cornelia explored further.

She looked into the drawing room and noted approvingly that the maroon draperies on the long, narrow windows were new and immaculate. A parlor in blues and greens looked homey and comfortable. The hallways were wide and accommodating. The floors were a gleaming parquet. Little Elizabeth, who was in leading strings now, would have plenty of room to roam and play.

"Look, Cornelia, we already have invitations awaiting us," Margaret said.

They did indeed. The silver salver atop the marble table in the hall contained a tidy stack of invitations. Cornelia had written to relatives and girlhood friends to let them know of her visit. Frederick's mother, while disapproving of the journey, had nevertheless done her duty by contacting acquaintances on Cornelia's behalf. Margaret had contacts as well, so the Season should not be without plenty of diversion.

Good. Cornelia was ready for some diversion from thoughts of Frederick. Reflecting back on her marriage always led to sadness. She had thought she and Frederick were happy together and that she knew and understood him perfectly. In the light of hindsight, she realized she had deceived herself. And he had deceived her.

She recalled how many times he had ridden out at night offering her only vague explanations. She had not questioned him because she had trusted him. And how many times had she assumed he was consulting with the estate manager late in the evening when he had actually been occupied with other things? she wondered.

To keep her bitterness from deepening, Cornelia tried to distract herself with other thoughts. The ones that came most frequently to mind were remembrances of the fair. That also brought thoughts of Edwin Sorrels. What had happened to him? Had he recovered?

"Isn't it perfect?" Margaret called from the top of the stairway.

"Yes, it is. We are going to have a famous time here."

She was going to enjoy herself in her first Season in London. Nothing was going to get in the way of that.

Four days after her arrival in London, Cornelia rode in her carriage on the way to a banquet in honor of an aging and distant cousin of Frederick's. Across from her, Margaret sat calmly while Cornelia fiddled with her high fichu collar.

"Is something wrong with the collar?" her companion inquired gently.

Cornelia sighed. "No. I'm nervous."

"Why? You know several people who will be at the banquet."

"Yes." But she still felt nervous. "It's been a long time since I attended a social event as an unmarried woman. And I have never done so in London."

Margaret smiled. "You must relax. I am persuaded you shall enjoy yourself immeasurably."

The carriage stopped. Cornelia took a deep breath

and followed Margaret out. She walked up the steps to the large, Georgian-style house with all the enthusiasm of a woman going to her execution. Frederick's cousin Rosaline was waiting for her just inside the door.

"Cornelia, how good to see you!"

The two women embraced and Cornelia presented Margaret.

Rosaline, plump from bearing four children, put a motherly arm around Cornelia. "You must let me introduce you to everyone."

Inside of fifteen minutes, it felt as if Rosaline had indeed introduced Cornelia and Margaret to every person present. Cornelia's head swam with the list of names. She could not possibly connect a name with the dizzying array of faces.

The tall, older gentleman who came up to her while she stood alone must have realized that. "I am Lord Bettonbrook, in case you don't recall," he said courteously.

She smiled at him, grateful for his thoughtfulness. "I must own I have become a bit confused with names."

"I can see how that might be so." He smiled reassuringly back at her. "There are so many to learn all at once."

"Yes," she murmured.

Cornelia recognized his look of masculine interest and felt flattered. She judged him to be twenty years older than she, and he seemed a bit stuffy, but he was amiable.

Over the course of the evening Lord Bettonbrook proved very attentive to her. He brought her a glass of punch and stood up with her twice. More than that would have been inappropriate, but she thought he would like to have stood up with her again. It was nice to have a man pay attention to her. She ended up enjoying the evening very much and was sorry to see it end.

"Did you have a good time?" Cornelia asked Margaret on the way home. The question was really posed as an opening to tell about her own evening.

"Yes. I won a modest amount at faro from some sweet dowagers who had very little skill at cards."

"You took their money!"

"Of course I did." Margaret patted her net reticule lovingly. "I would not like to have made them look like objects of pity by refusing my winnings."

"You're wicked."

"I daresay you have the right of it," Margaret agreed placidly, her hand still affectionately touching the reticule.

Cornelia could not help but smile at her companion's unrepentance. It was difficult to be out of humour long with Margaret. She was not always kind, but she was always amusing.

"If it makes you feel better, I shall probably have fierce indigestion tomorrow," Margaret told her. "I ate far too much of the punch and cake. You must tell me about your own evening."

Cornelia gladly did.

Margaret's prediction was right. Cornelia was summoned to her friend's sitting room the following morning to find her reclining on the sofa looking perfectly miserable.

"Have you something that will cure me?"

Cornelia snapped open her bag. "Let me see. Here's powdered colomba root, carbonate of soda and ground ginder. That's everything I need to make a cure."

"Good."

While Cornelia was busy mixing a drachm of each, Margaret pulled herself up on the sofa and said wanly, "I've a letter to send to Walter. Could you post it?"

"Of course." Walter was Margaret's brother the vicar. Neither had ever married, and the pair were very devoted to each other. In the short time she had been in London, Margaret had written to him several times. He had also written to her.

"I am almost out of powdered colomba root," Cornelia noted. "I shall have to find a shop that sells herbs." Already word of her skill was spreading among the neighbor's servants. Those from nearby households had begun calling at her kitchen door to ask for cures.

"I'll put this in milk and you are to take some three times a day," Cornelia instructed.

Margaret nodded weakly. As Cornelia started from the room, she pressed, "You *will* mail the letter today, won't you?"

"Yes, of course." Such devotion between brother and sister was surprising but refreshing, Cornelia reflected as she went down the steps with the letter in hand. She put the thought aside as she made a mental list of the herbs she needed to buy.

Two days later Lord Bettonbrook came to call. He appeared again the following day.

"You have an admirer," a recovered Margaret teased her. "And a marquis at that. I hear he is not so wealthy, but his pockets are not entirely to let. For a widow with a child, he would make a splendid catch."

"It's too early to be thinking of marriage," Cornelia informed her primly.

The two women's eyes met, and Cornelia could not suppress a smile. "You have the right of it. I have been thinking that very thing myself, but we shall have to wait and see how matters progress."

"Don't wait to see, you peagoose. You must *make* things progress."

"I fail to see how one does that." Frederick had courted her. She had never cast out lures for a man.

"By smiling and batting those long lashes and looking very prettily up at him."

"I'm a mature woman, not a simpering girl," Cornelia informed her crisply. "Besides, I am not at all sure I am interested in a match." When she considered her marriage to Frederick and how disappointed she had been in all that she had learned about it, she wondered why she should ever want to get married again. Certainly if she did remarry, it would be a match of convenience and not one of love. She was too wise to fall in love at this stage in her life.

"I think you are being coy. You like him."

It was true that she did enjoy the attention. After having had her confidence undermined by Frederick's mother, it was refreshing to know that someone found her attractive.

Lord Bettonbrook continued to call, and a week later she was invited to attend an affair as his guest.

She spent a good deal of time fretting over what to wear.

Margaret finally persuaded her that the navy bombazine trimmed with gauze with its high, scalloped neckline was her most becoming choice. "You should have your hair cut, too, in a Grecian style."

Cornelia touched her matronly bun indecisively. "That is for younger women."

Margaret spread her hands in exasperation. "If you wish to look older than your years, that is up to you. But you have a pretty face and an excellent figure. You could make yourself more appealing."

"Perhaps," she said vaguely and retired to her dressing room intent on keeping her hair in its same demure bun.

Her Irish maid Beth worked diligently to style it thus. Alas, the night was humid, and Cornelia's hair curled more than usual. It persisted in escaping from its pins into springy, rebellious brown tendrils that floated around her oval face flirtatiously.

Cornelia surveyed herself in the cheval glass and bit her lip. "Dear me, what's to be done, Beth?"

"It is not your usual style, ma'am, but I find it fetching."

Cornelia paled. "I'm a widow, Beth. I should look proper and dignified—not 'fetching.' " Besides, this style made her look even younger than her five-and-twenty years, making the contrast between her age and Lord Bettonbrook's even more marked.

The maid renewed her efforts to calm the playful curls but finally was forced to step back and concede, "I'm afraid there's not much to be done, ma'am, and it's time for you to go."

Cornelia sighed. "I guess this will have to do." Rising, she picked up her kid gloves and started toward the door.

Lord Bettonbrook was looking at his watch when she arrived downstairs.

"Am I late?" she asked breathlessly.

He consulted the watch again. "Six minutes," he determined.

"I'm sorry."

The marquis led her wordlessly outside.

His waiting carriage was not large and grand, but it had a small, distinctive crest on it, and the horses were nicely matched sorrels. He handed her inside and climbed in after her. The footman closed the door. The carriage lurched gently and began to move forward.

Lord Bettonbrook was clearly more particular about time than Frederick had been, but punctuality was a very good virtue to have, she told herself.

They arrived at the party less than ten minutes later. It was a formal event with a long receiving line. As Cornelia moved through the line, she recognized several people. She smiled at a dowager and nodded to a debutante. She was almost at the end of the receiving line when she stopped abruptly.

The man in front of her lifted a limp hand and fixed her with a bored smile. He was dressed in dandified mustard yellow breeches, a white waistcoat, and a cravat folded in elaborate and overblown intricacies. He regarded her through a quizzing glass. "How do you do?" he inquired with great ennui. The accent was strongly aristocratic.

She looked closer. "You're Edwin Sorrels."

"I'm afraid you have mistaken me for someone else. I am Lord Taveston," he said in the same bored, high-born accent.

Cornelia blinked and stood mute.

Lord Bettonbrook handled the introductions. "Lord Taveston, may I present Lady Devenish."

"Charmed to meet you." It was a disinterested, perfunctory greeting. Edwin Sorrels was already turning to the person behind her.

Speechless, Cornelia allowed herself to be led along. She glanced back and saw that he had not even looked in her direction again. He seemed completely oblivious to her.

"I know that man," she whispered to the marquis. "His name is Edwin Sorrels."

Lord Bettonbrook shook his head. "No, my dear, that's the Earl of Taveston. A dreadful fop, I'm afraid, but of quite unexceptional birth."

Cornelia looked back again. Edwin Sorrels, whatever else he might have seemed last summer, had not been a fop. Even now she saw that his dandified clothes could not conceal the firm sinews of masculine legs nor the muscled spread of chest. What sort of deception was he perpetrating? *Was* he a lord or had he somehow managed to convince people he was? The awful thought occurred to her that he had killed the real Lord Taveston and was impersonating him.

She grasped Lord Bettonbrook's arm. "How long have you known this man?"

"Half a dozen years, I should think."

Half a dozen years, she repeated to herself. That still did not mean he was an earl, only that he might have been at the deception for some time.

"You look a little pale, my dear. Perhaps a glass of ratafia would make you feel more the thing."

"Yes, please." Lord Bettonbrook left, and Cornelia's gaze flitted back to the receiving line. Most of the guests had now arrived, and people in the line were breaking away to mingle with the rest of the guests. She watched Edwin Sorrels move out of the line. She was staring right at him, but he did not so much as look at her.

Surely he could not have failed to recognize her. Yet he had given no sign that he did. She began to doubt herself. Was it possible there were two men who looked as remarkably alike as Lord Taveston and Edwin Sorrels? They could have been twins.

Lord Bettonbrook returned with her drink. She sipped it absently as the musicians began to play the first dance of the evening. She was curious about Edwin Sorrels, but she could scarcely flit about the room quizzing people about him. For the moment, she was forced to contain her curiosity.

Cornelia stood up for the boulanger with Lord Bettonbrook and later danced with other men. Her partners were usually older—the young blades being occupied with vying for the attentions of this Season's crop of girls being presented. Not that she minded standing up with older men, but she would not object to being swept into a dance that left her breathless. Instead she was led decorously through the steps.

She was being escorted off the floor following another tame dance when Lord Taveston approached her. He stopped in front of her and surveyed her idly through his quizzing glass as her dance partner took his leave. "Lady Devenish, was it not?"

"Yes," she said with pursed lips.

"If you have a moment, I should like to speak privately with you."

Cornelia watched him through narrowed, suspicious eyes. She was certain he *was* Edwin Sorrels. What sort of game was he playing?

"On the balcony, if you please," Lord Taveston directed disinterestedly.

She was tempted to tell him no. But she did not want to deprive herself of the opportunity to give the blackguard an angry piece of her mind. To think she had actually worried about him after finding him hurt in the woods. Not only had he prowled through her house, but he had appeared there lying about his name.

They reached the end of the balcony. He stopped near a shrub that was clipped into the shape of a cat and turned to her. "It would please me if you would refrain from telling anyone that we had met previously, Lady Devenish."

"I was not altogether certain we *had* a previous encounter," she shot back tartly. "Earlier you looked at me as if I were a piece of the furniture."

"I very *charming* piece of the furniture," he said smoothly and insincerely.

Her flush was one of anger and not missish embarrassment. "Pray, spare me your meaningless compliments. I think it very bold of you to ask me for a favor. The last time I saw you, you were lying in wet grass with a gash in your head—probably a well-deserved gash," she added to quell his obnoxious smile. "You didn't even have the decency to

78

send me word that you had recovered after I attended to your injury."

"Circumstances made that difficult." He glanced toward the window and then drew her further into the shadow of the cat-shaped shrub. His hand on her arm was firm, and he became brisk and businesslike as he continued, "It is a matter of some urgency that you tell no one you saw me last summer at your estate."

Cornelia watched him coolly. "Urgency? Forgive me, milord, if I find it passing difficult to believe you." In light of the discovery of Frederick's deceptions, it was hard for Cornelia to have faith in any man. She particularly had no reason to believe this man. "As for the intrigue in which you are quite obviously embroiled, I do not wish to know anything more about it."

His hand on her upper arm tightened enough to remind her that he might be dressed like a harmless dandy, but he had the strength of two men. "I would strongly advise you to follow my counsel and keep your tongue inside your head, Lady Devenish."

Cornelia hated herself for flinching under his icy stare. He looked full of menacing purpose. Looking at him now, she could not help but wonder what he might be capable of. He continued to hold her arm with enough pressure to unnerve her.

She tried for haughty composure. "You are hurting my arm, sir. Pray let me go."

He released her but kept her rooted to the spot by the sheer force of his gaze. "Lives may be at stake here."

"Yes, but how do I know if they are English lives or French lives?" she countered.

79

His voice grew more reasonable as he continued, "Cornelia, Frederick was killed by someone who waylaid him on a dark road. If he had been suspected of spying for Napoleon he would have been tried and hanged for treason to make an example of him."

"That proves only that my husband was not a traitor, not what you are."

"I came to Devon to see Frederick. I would scarcely have done so if we had been enemies, would I?" he asked reasonably.

"You didn't even know he was dead," she challenged. "Surely a friend would have known."

"I had been—" he paused before concluding, "—out of the country."

He was persuasive, she would give him that. As much as she hated to admit it, his arguments were logical and sounded credible.

He must have sensed that. "I am glad we have reached an understanding. Now we must return to the party before tongues begin to wag."

Cornelia's thoughts were jumbled as Lord Taveston pulled her back toward the door. There was nothing of the fop in his bearing now, she noted through her distraction. If anything he was all raw virility and confidence. At the door, however, that changed abruptly. He entered the room looking every inch the overdressed dandy.

"There you are, my dear." Lord Bettonbrook appeared at her elbow. "Was that Lord Taveston you were with?"

"Yes."

He looked as if he were full of questions and perhaps a hint of jealousy, but she was grateful that he did not pursue the matter. She had enough on her mind at the moment without coming up with lies about what they had discussed. Thankfully, he led her out to dance and she did not see Lord Taveston the rest of the evening. She hoped she did not run into him the remainder of the time she was in London.

Chapter 6

As if to thwart her wishes, Cornelia seemed to meet Lord Taveston at every turn. Over the next days, she saw him at the opera, in Hyde Park, and at Vauxhall Gardens.

Cornelia was in a satin-draped box with Lord Bettonbrook at Drury Lane when she again spied Lord Taveston. He was in the company of a beautiful, sultry-looking woman who was possessed of cleavage, flashing eyes, and coy smile. Cornelia glanced self-consciously down at her prim silver-gray gown, then brought herself up short. How foolish to worry about her clothes. They were perfectly respectable. They might not compete with the clothes worn by the other woman, but she was not in competition, she reminded herself.

Leaning toward Lord Bettonbrook, Cornelia inquired as casually as possible. "Who is that accompanying Lord Taveston?"

He glanced in the direction she indicated. "Lady Jane."

"I do not believe I have met her." She would definitely have remembered a woman of such beauty.

"She has just returned from a trip to the North."

Cornelia sat back and fluttered her feather fan across her cheeks. What sort of relationship did Lady Jane have with Lord Taveston? She had heard enough London gossip to know that many women of high birth entertained men in their beds. Did she and Edwin . . . ?

Cornelia straightened abruptly. It was beneath her to consider such matters. Turning toward Lord Bettonbrook, she said tersely, "I find the weather tolerably warm these days, don't you?"

"Quite so."

Cornelia resolved not to look in Lord Taveston's direction the remainder of the night.

Lord Taveston smiled with faint amusement at something Lady Jane had whispered in his ear. Without ever appearing to do so, he kept an eye on Cornelia. She was with Bettonbrook again, he noted. The marquis was not a bad sort, but he was far too old for her.

Matches between old men and younger women took place all the time, but the earl did not believe Cornelia would be happy with someone so staid as Bettonbrook. One had only to look at Emma Hamilton, who had forsaken her elderly husband for Lord Nelson, to know that such matches did not work with women of spirit. And Lady Devenish did have a certain spirit.

Not that her personal life mattered a whit to him, he reminded himself. He was only interested in her insofar as she could help him. Because of Frederick's death and the loss of the list of prominent British who were spying for the French, it was necessary for him to rediscover who the traitors were. He was in London suffering through the Season for precisely that purpose.

"You are not attending to me."

He glanced up to see Lady Jane pouting. "How churlish of me," he murmured, taking her hand and kissing it with lingering attention.

"That's better," she all but purred.

Edwin again kissed her wrist. There were worse things than caressing the soft skin of a beautiful woman, he consoled himself. It was certainly better than hiding in a barn near Calais waiting for a boat to rescue him while he listened to the hounds drawing nearer. Still, his dalliance with Lady Jane was for the purpose of unmasking the high-placed traitors and not because he felt any particular passion for her.

There were others of rank working with him, but meetings between them were rare. Most of his communications took place through coded messages and oblique conversation at parties.

His gaze trailed back to Cornelia. Did she have any information that could help him? he wondered. And if she did, could he cajole her into sharing it with him?

She looked in his direction and their eyes met. Instantly she lifted her chin and turned away.

It did not appear his chances of charming anything out of Cornelia were good, he acknowledged regretfully. It was plain that she disliked him thoroughly.

A pity. He would have to see if he could change that, because he might be able to use her. He did feel a pull of regret at the thought of using Cornelia. After all, she was a widow, and she had already suffered much. But Edwin could not allow softer feelings to get in his way if Lady Devenish could be a means to an end.

Word of Cornelia's skill with herbs continued to spread; people came to her in ever greater numbers. She was pleased that they did. Many of them were too poor to afford a doctor and would go without medical attention if she did not see them.

At home she had her own herb garden, and she dried herbs for the winter months. She had been able to replenish her dwindling supply of medicinals by sending back to Devon for them. But she was again in need of more. This time, she must try to find a place in London to buy them, Cornelia noted as she walked into the kitchen to attend to the man waiting there on a wooden bench.

The stout man wearing a stocking cap was the third person she had seen this week who had influenza. She used the last of her senna and syrup of poppies in making a mixture for him.

When Lord Bettonbrook called on her later that afternoon, she asked if he knew of a shop that sold herbs.

"I have passed one now and again."

"Can you give me the direction?"

"I could take you there," he offered stiffly.

That was exactly what she had wanted to hear. "If you're sure it is no trouble." She was already rising to get her shawl.

The air was so warm out that she scarcely needed the light shawl she had thrown over her rust-colored gown. Inside the marquis's carriage, the air felt close and lifeless with the windows up.

"Would you not like a breeze?" she suggested.

"Too much fresh air is bad for the lungs."

"Oh." Cornelia fell silent. She had always liked being out in the air. She did not even mind acquiring a few freckles, although she knew it was most unfashionable for a lady to have them. But she did not argue with Lord Bettonbrook.

The shop was less than a half hour's drive away.

Cornelia stepped inside the little corner store and let her eyes adjust to the dim light. The scent of ginger and sage and rosemary greeted her. Plants hung from the ceiling drying; one wall was lined with bins containing dried herbs. On a neat bookshelf sat copies of Buchan's *Domestic Remedies* and John Wesley's *Primitive Physic or an Easy and Natural Method of Curing Most Diseases*. The shop felt cozy and friendly, and she was inclined to linger.

A tiny woman shuffled forward and offered her assistance.

"I have a list of things I need," Cornelia said, "but I would like to look first."

"Of course." The shopkeeper retreated.

Lord Bettonbrook stood by the door while Cornelia lifted the wooden lid to a bin and peeked inside, closing her eyes to inhale the sweet scent of lavender. "Come smell this," she coaxed Lord Bettonbrook.

He moved cautiously forward and obliged her with a brief sniff. Then he straightened and retreated to the door.

It was difficult to relax and enjoy the setting

when he was standing waiting for her, so Cornelia turned her attention to selecting her purchases.

The shopkeeper helped her measure out quantities of several varieties of herbs and even gave her a different version of Huxham's tincture. The woman seemed very knowledgeable, and Cornelia wished she could have stayed to chat with her, but she sensed her escort's impatience.

"I'm ready," Cornelia finally announced.

Lord Bettonbrook was quick to open the door.

She must not be offended that he displayed little interest in the shop, Cornelia told herself. If he had taken her to one of his clubs or male haunts, she would have felt equally out of place.

Besides, she should not expect a man to understand her need to tend those less fortunate. Frederick had been only lukewarm in his support of her work. She was learning to temper her expectations of men, even those she had toward a possible future husband.

The role of women in this world, she had discovered to her pain, was not to be happy but to get by with the least amount of heartache. That was why Bettonbrook was a reasonable choice. She liked him, but she recognized she did not have a grand passion for him. An overwhelming passion was something she hoped never to experience again. One could not be disappointed if one did not have such high expectations.

It was Margaret who first heard about the sale at the Bittermore house.

"I've not heard they are having a sale," Cornelia had said.

"Very few know it yet."

"You always know what is going on among the London ton. You must listen at keyholes," Cornelia teased.

Margaret bristled. "I scarcely think that knowing a few things implies I go around listening at keyholes."

The sharpness of Margaret's reaction surprised her. "I was only joking. I did not mean to offend."

Margaret unbent slightly. "I don't like the inference, even in jest."

"I do apologize," she said and then tried to change the subject. "It seems dreadful to take advantage of the Bittermore's misfortune by buying their possessions."

"My dear naive Cornelia, they *need* people to buy their things so that they may pay off their debts. Of course it's very sad, but if Mr. Bittermore speculated on the Exchange unwisely, there is really no one to blame for that but himself. We are not the cause of his troubles. It is said they have some beautiful crystal and some lovely oriental vases. You ought to at least go and have a look."

Cornelia finally agreed to go but only with the intention of looking.

The wind was mild outside, and the sun was shining through the windows of the small but elegant house when they arrived. They had come early to inspect the library, plate, wardrobe, and wine cellar before the auction began.

Unfortunately, half of London had come with the same purpose. The house was so crowded that it became a feat to squeeze from room to room. She and Margaret were soon separated.

In the dining room Cornelia found herself wedged between two stout matrons who were examining the Limoges china and sparkling crystal with gimlet eyes. Any flaw was bound to be spotted.

The china was pretty but Cornelia had no special interest in it. She was about to move on to another room when she spied a pair of gold candlesticks. She skirted past a young buck to inspect them more closely. They were painstakingly carved to look like miniature Greek columns. Cornelia had a good pair of silver candlesticks at home, but these captured her heart. She touched one with a careful finger. She wanted them.

Margaret reappeared. "There you are. I'm going upstairs. Do you wish to come?"

"No." She did not leave the dining room.

As a wizened auctioneer took his place at the table with his ivory hammer, Cornelia made up her mind to buy the golden treasures. She knew that some ladies did their own bidding, but she hired one of the oriental men roaming the house to bid for her.

"How much is?" he asked in his fractured English.

Cornelia named a sum that was twice what a sane person would pay. But she had fallen in love with the candlesticks, and no price seemed too high. Heavy with anticipation, she made her way to a chair and sat down.

While she waited impatiently for the auction to start, she saw several people she recognized. She had just exchanged greetings with Lord Windwood when she saw Lord Taveston edging through the throng. He was fastidiously dressed in a sage green cut-away coat and white unmentionables.

He nodded to her from across the room. She returned a distant answering nod and looked away. Images of him at Drury Lane with the beautiful Lady Jane made her feel cool toward him. It was not, of course, that she was jealous—merely that she wished to have no association with him.

"My good friends, we are ready to begin," the auctioneer announced in a bass voice that surprised her coming from so shriveled a man.

People continued to try to crowd into the already full dining room. They overflowed out the open double doors into the hallway, the kitchen, and the drawing room. Margaret squeezed through the crowd and sat beside Cornelia in the chair she had saved.

"Number One is a portrait of two children. Who'll bid for it?" the auctioneer asked.

The gold candlesticks were Number 367. Cornelia folded her arms and prepared for a wait.

Across the room Lord Taveston had found a place along the wall to lean against. As the auction progressed, he bid on some fine burgundy and later on a marble statue. From time to time he glanced at Cornelia. When she looked at him at all, it was with coldness.

He wished to change that. The situation was getting tenser with the French. There were rumors of a massive build up along the coast. There could be only one reason for that. They were preparing to invade England. He and his associates must stop the flow of information to the French by finding out which British aristocrats were spies.

Cornelia might be able to help him. Frederick may have let fall some information that could be useful. At any rate, it could not hurt to cultivate a friendship with her rather than this hostility. To prove he was a decent fellow, he would buy her something, he decided. He could tell her it was a gift for having tended his wound. A gift would surely soften her and pave the way to him asking her about details, however small, that Frederick might have let drop in her presence. It had not escaped Edwin's notice how longingly Cornelia had looked at the gold candlesticks. If she did not bid on them herself, he would buy them for her.

"Number three hundred sixty-three, a wine decanter," the auctioneer announced.

Cornelia leaned forward and drummed her fingers impatiently on the arm of her chair. Time dragged on. At last they were almost up to the candlesticks.

Number 365 sold and then Number 366. Finally the auctioneer was ready to begin bidding on Number 367.

Margaret smiled encouragingly at her.

The price began low but a dismaying number of people held up cards to bid.

"Fifteen. Who'll give more? Sixteen."

Cornelia's oriental man bid steadily and solemnly. He never looked in her direction. As the price climbed, people dropped out.

"Twenty-one. Who'll give twenty-two?"

"There are only two people remaining," Margaret murmured.

Cornelia looked around to see who the other bidder was. Lord Taveston held up his card.

She stared resentfully at him.

Undaunted, he continued to bid. The price rose to thirty.

"Really, Cornelia," Margaret leaned over to whisper, "Thirty pounds is entirely too high."

"I don't care." She looked darkly toward Lord Taveston and felt her blood pressure rise as he smiled back at her. "What cheek," she muttered.

"Perhaps he wants the candlesticks for one of his estates. I hear he has a magnificent house not far from Bath."

"He is doing this to keep me from buying them," Cornelia said waspishly.

"How can he possibly know you are bidding on them?"

"He can see I am unhappy with him, and yet he does not quit bidding."

"He doesn't know that you are annoyed with him," Margaret said.

Cornelia was in no frame of mind to be logical.

Across the room, Lord Taveston was more determined than ever to buy the candlesticks after seeing the distraught glances Lady Devenish cast toward him. She clearly wanted them but was too shy to bid for them in a public place. He glanced toward her and inclined his head with a smile of reassurance.

She looked away.

The ivory gavel came down on the table. "Sold to Lord Taveston for thirty-five pounds."

Margaret patted her hand comfortingly. "Do you wish to leave?"

"Yes." She rose abruptly. The two women threaded their way through the crowded room toward the door. Once outside, Cornelia stalked toward her carriage. She would have been annoyed at anyone who bought the candlesticks. The fact that it was Lord Taveston was doubly irritating, especially after seeing him smile at her. Was he taunting her?

"Lady Devenish." She glanced back across the street to see the earl descending the stairs of the house. She swung away from him and stepped up into her carriage.

Margaret hesitated. "Cornelia, Lord Taveston is trying to speak to you."

"I do not have anything to say to him."

Margaret stood irresolutely in the open door. A moment later she stepped aside and Lord Taveston's tall frame took up the doorway. "Lady Devenish, I didn't want you to leave without—"

"I am in a great hurry, milord," she cut him off rudely. Any sensitive man would have taken the hint. But he stood there obstinately and added insult to injury by raising his right hand to show her the candlesticks.

"I had the devil of a time buying these." He grinned. "I thought the Chinaman would never stop bidding. They're quite a handsome pair."

She met this statement with cold silence.

He seemed to falter, then continued, "I had seen you admiring them earlier and thought you wanted them. I hope that you will accept them from me as a gesture of goodwill and—"

"Lord Taveston, I really haven't the time to . . ." Her words dwindled away. She blinked. "Accept them?" He was indeed holding the beautiful gold candlesticks toward her.

"Yes, in appreciation for a certain favor you did for me."

She knew he meant the night she had gone to him in the forest when he was injured.

He pressed the candlesticks into her hands.

She looked down at them in confusion. "Th-thank you," she murmured.

"I know you are in a hurry, so I will not detain you longer." He handed Margaret into the carriage and bowed to both of them before disappearing.

Moments later the two women were rolling along Oxford Street.

Cornelia sat in embarrassed silence, regretting all the unkind things she had said about the earl.

Margaret eyed her speculatively. "How very generous of him."

"Yes."

"Do you think he has a score for you?"

"Of course not," she denied quickly.

"It was an expensive gift for one as loosely acquainted as the pair of you seem to be. Unless there is something I don't know about." The last sentence hung in the air like a question.

"He saw me admiring them earlier," Cornelia said by way of weak explanation and then fell to arranging the folds of her skirt.

"Hmmm. Lord Taveston puts me in mind of someone I have seen before, but I cannot remember where."

Margaret had attended the fair last summer and probably remembered him from there. But it had been a crowded event so it was little wonder she had trouble recalling him.

"You were not acquainted with him before?" Margaret asked.

Cornelia ran a hand gently along the side of one

of the candlesticks. "No, I have never seen him before this Season." After buying her such a lovely and expensive gift, she would certainly honor the silence he had asked of her.

Margaret continued to watch her closely. Finally, she said, "Well, it was nice of him to buy them for you. You must invite him over for tea and thank him properly."

"Yes, I suppose I should."

As the carriage swayed gently onward, Cornelia retreated into her own thoughts. Why had the earl gone to so much trouble and expense to buy a present for her? Was it truly in appreciation for her help as he had said? She did not know.

In truth she knew very little about him. He was a chameleon. Like the performer he had played on stage last year, he was capable of acting any part. She had already seen him play the rustic, the fop, and the earnest aristocrat. Which was the real Edwin Sorrels?

Not that it really ought to matter to her. She certainly had no romantic interest in the earl. She was being called on by a man who was a much better match than the unpredictable earl would ever be.

Lord Bettonbrook sent flowers to Cornelia the following morning. They were long-stemmed red roses that looked exquisite in an oriental vase. Cornelia had placed them on the mantle in the parlor. They added fragrance to the room of blues and greens.

"Are you thinking of marrying him?" Margaret demanded as the two women sat in the parlor plying their needles.

"He has not asked me," Cornelia replied demurely.

Margaret smirked. "Don't come the innocent with me. You know very well he is courting you and that he will come up to scratch. Do you wish to marry him?"

Cornelia had already asked herself that question."He would be a good father. He has never had children, but he displays a gratifying interest in Elizabeth." He always enquired after her daughter's health even though he had declined Cornelia's invitations to accompany her to the nursery to look in on the sleeping child.

"It seems only a matter of time before he proposes," Margaret observed.

"I think Lord Bettonbrook and I would rub along well together," Cornelia said thoughtfully. "He is older and very sensible." She put aside the thought of how awkward he had made her feel in the herb shop and concentrated on his good points. "It is true he laughs very little, but he is thoughtful and attentive and excessively well read. That is a good deal more in common than many couples enjoy."

"That is all very well, but I wonder if he could ever be fiery or passionate during those intimate moments a man and woman share."

Cornelia stuck herself with her needle. "Don't be absurd, Margaret. Who would want such a creature as that?" And what an odd statement for a vicar's maiden sister to make.

Margaret fell back to her needlework and both women were silent. It would not be proper for Cornelia to quiz Margaret on what she knew about passion, but the question did sit in her mind. Margaret could sometimes show a sense of humor that was almost bawdy. At other times she could take pious offense at some imagined insult. All in all, though, she was an unexceptional companion, and Cornelia much preferred her to being home with Frederick's mother.

An hour later the Horaby sisters, Ethel and Caroline, stopped in for a visit. They brought their little dog which sat on Ethel's spinster lap and barked at anyone who looked at it.

"Such a sweet dog," Margaret murmured with an insincere smile.

"Is it not?" Ethel agreed.

The conversation for the next few minutes revolved around the antics of the dog. They rapidly became tedious. Cornelia was relieved to hear the butler's footsteps.

"Lord Bettonbrook," he intoned in important accents.

The marquis entered the room and executed a precise bow to each woman. Then he sat on the green camelback sofa near Cornelia. She attempted not to speculate on Margaret's question about how passionate or fiery he might be in more intimate moments.

The conversation followed its usual course about the weather and upcoming social events.

It was during a lull in the talk that Ethel, the elder of the gray-haired sisters, pointed toward the gold candlesticks on the mantle. "How charming. Aren't they, Caroline?"

"Indeed," the quieter sister agreed.

The dog growled.

"Are they brass? They look as if they're gold."

"They are," Cornelia said.

"How precious. Wouldn't a pair like that make a perfect wedding gift for Mary's daughter, Caroline? You must tell me where you bought them, dear Cornelia."

"They were a gift," Cornelia said.

At the same moment, Margaret said, "She got them at the Bittermore auction."

Ethel looked from Cornelia to Margaret. The dog looked, too.

"They were sold at the Bittermore auction," Cornelia explained, "but I did not buy them there."

"I see." Ethel obviously did not.

"Lord Taveston bought them," Margaret explained further and then fell guiltily silent under Cornelia's quelling stare.

"And presented them to you, Margaret?" Ethel pressed.

Margaret studied her fingernails. "Not precisely."

"He gave them to me," Cornelia said to end further probing. She could feel Lord Bettonbrook's startled gaze upon her.

"You accepted such a gift from Lord Taveston?" he asked in chilling accents.

"Yes." Lord Bettonbrook's expression hardened with disapproval. The Hornaby sisters watched the interchange with delight, clearly glad that they had chosen this morning for their visit.

Cornelia attempted to turn the conversation to something less controversial, but the tension remained. Lord Bettonbrook, although he continued to look stiff and hurt, made valiant work of piecing together a conversation with Cornelia about the wonderful play showing at Drury Lane.

But no one else joined in and eventually that dwindled off into silence.

The marquis then tried to include a silent Margaret in the conversation.

"I have an aunt on my mother's side who lives at Dunsmore, Miss Simpson. I recollect a family by the name of Simpson living there. Would that be your family?"

"Yes."

"I believe my aunt once said something about the family taking in a child whose mother had died."

Margaret inclined her head in a way that neither confirmed nor denied his statement.

"A boy of about ten, was it not?"

"Yes." She added nothing further.

Lord Bettonbrook did not remain long before taking his departure. Cornelia watched him go with an unhappy feeling. How displeased was he about her accepting a gift from another man? Would he even continue to call on her?

The Hornaby woman left reluctantly a short time after. The dog cast a final parting snarl back into the room before being carried out.

"We shall see you at Lady Hauserman's tonight," Caroline called back to them. "She always has the most amusing evenings."

"Yes, I look forward to seeing you again tonight," Cornelia said with a weak smile.

Once they were alone, she turned to Margaret. "Lord Bettonbrook was very upset with me."

"Not to put too fine a point on it, but I should say he was jealous."

Cornelia nodded ruefully. "Whatever was I thinking to accept anything from Lord Taveston?

I don't even like the man. It is Lord Bettonbrook
that I have formed an attachment to." She hoped
Lord Taveston did not respond to the invitation
she had felt obliged to send him asking him to
call.

Chapter 7

Edwin rapped at the door of Cornelia's house with the silver knob of his cane. It was a morning full of sun and singing birds and a splendid day for riding in the park. He was foregoing that pleasure to call on Cornelia. Her invitation to visit presented an opportunity he did not wish to pass up.

She had been a widow over a year now. The pain of her husband's death was no longer so fresh. Now he could ask her questions about Frederick's final days.

Lord Taveston was just getting ready to knock again when the door was opened by a crisp servant.

He presented his card and was directed to a parlor of blue with strong green accents. He recalled that Lady Sarah, a woman he had once known, had liked this same combination of colors. He picked a comfortable chair and settled in to wait. Lady Sarah was married to a duke now. Edwin wondered if she had redecorated the old ducal pile in Wilshire over in blues and greens.

She had wanted him to marry her. Edwin's sisters had found the idea most appealing and had told him so. His father had thought it a capital idea.

"Time you had some brats," had been the exact paternal words. Even Edwin's valet had believed it a good idea and had been even more conscientious in his duties during the time of Lady Sarah. For a while it had seemed to Edwin that he was the only one who did not think the match a good idea.

Not that the lady had not been eminently suitable. On the contrary, she had been bright and beautiful and charming. But he had not longed for her when he was away from her, and her name hadn't fallen from his lips when he was riding along lonely roads at night.

The truth was he had no need of a wife. He had other obligations that were more important. What need had a man of a wife when he could be of service to his country? A smile tugged at his mouth as he acknowledged that sometimes in the smallest hours of the night, a woman made a better companion than honorable thoughts of one's country. But ladies could always be found to supply warmth when needed.

From out of nowhere came the vague recollection of a woman stroking his hair. He remembered lying on cold ground and feeling a terrible throbbing in his head. He recalled being unable to open his eyes and hearing the soft murmur of a woman's voice. Gentle fingers touched his neck. The memory of that touch and the feeling of safety it had evoked awakened a silent need. He resolutely pushed that thought aside. Men became weak when they became dependent on women. His strength was in his own ability to rely on himself.

He glanced at the door as it opened and Cornelia stepped into the room. She was tall but she moved with grace and quietness, like a willow in a breeze.

Her dark gown flowed with her movements. The color of her dress was too somber, he noted, and wondered what she would look like in a gown of bright red. He liked the picture he conjured up for himself.

Smiling pleasantly, he rose and bowed to her. "Good morning, Lady Devenish."

"Good morning, milord."

She held herself tightly. He realized he would have to put her at ease if he meant to glean information about Frederick. He was thankful that he finally had some time alone with her.

"Lady Devenish, I am aware that—"

The door behind her opened again and another lady entered. He cursed silently.

"Lord Taveston, have you met my friend, Miss Simpson?"

"No, I have not had the pleasure." He moved forward to bow over her hand. His bored smile hid his irritation at this unexpected presence.

The three of them sat on blue chairs and green sofas and discussed the weather and the latest opera. It was plain Cornelia had asked Margaret to join them because she did not wish to be alone with him. Annoyed, he settled back in his chair. Lady Devenish smoothed her skirts and tucked back strands of her hair into a bun more suited to an older woman. She should wear her curls short and free.

Margaret was speaking. "We have had many lovely compliments on the candlesticks, Lord Taveston. They were quite a charming gift."

"Yes," Cornelia said stiffly. "I wish to thank you for them."

Then why didn't she look at him and smile? She

had a pretty smile, and she showed it all too seldom. At least to him. It occurred to him he had seen her to be more winsome to Lord Bettonbrook. Once during a contradance, she had made a misstep and had laughed with such guileless charm that he had almost lost his own step in watching her.

"I'm glad you like them," he said with languid smoothness. He watched Cornelia touch the skirts of her gown and again considered the merits of presenting her with a red frock. The impropriety of such a gift might be overshadowed by the pleasure of seeing her in something with color.

There was a short silence between the three of them. "I find the weather very pleasant these days," Cornelia finally said.

A strained conversation about the weather ensued. The visit was not going at all as Edwin had wished.

"Where are you from?" Miss Simpson asked.

"I have property near Bath and a little in London."

"I have spent most of my time in Devon so I know so few people," she said lightly.

He had the impression that the statement was made for the purpose of drawing more information out of him. He only smiled vacantly and sharpened the crease of his cravat with his fingers.

"Have you ever traveled in Devon, milord?"

"No. I must make a point of doing so sometime."

"Yes. It is very lovely." She looked distracted, as if she were struggling to think of something. He wondered if she had seen him in Devon and was trying to place him. If so, she was clearly failing.

He was making no progress here in questioning Cornelia. He might as well leave. He was reaching for his silver-tipped cane when a servant appeared and whispered to Cornelia.

She rose quickly. "No, I shall go immediately." Turning to the earl, she said, "I pray you will excuse me, milord, but one of the Halsey's servants has taken ill, and I have been asked to come." She was all brisk and purposeful now. "Have the carriage put to, Giles. Tell Robert to hurry."

"I can take you, Lady Devenish," Lord Taveston offered.

"I wouldn't wish to impose—"

"My carriage is already waiting at the door. It will be faster than having yours sent round."

That decided her. "Very well. Margaret, do you wish to join me?"

"Thank you, no. The sight of sick people makes me queasy."

Lord Taveston was glad to hear that.

It was a matter of moments before Cornelia had gathered a brown pelisse around her and grabbed a black bag. Then she was seated beside him on the crimson velvet squabs of his carriage.

He gave his driver directions to the Halsey's. "Quickly," he admonished.

The young, enthusiastic driver took him at his word. They set a fair pace down Charing Cross road and rounded a corner with enough speed to tilt the carriage. Cornelia slid against him and Edwin felt the warmth and suppleness of her body.

"I beg your pardon," she murmured. She was trying to move back to her place when the carriage spun around another corner, and she was again in his lap. She blushed. "I'm *very* sorry, Lord Taveston."

"Stop apologizing." He put a steadying hand

around her shoulder and kept it there. "It promises to be a turbulent ride and you are going to continue to be jolted up next to me. You can comfort yourself with the knowledge we are going so fast the journey won't take long."

A weak smile touched her lips. "I daresay you have the right of it. But by the time we arrive, *we* may be more in need of medical attention than the Halsey's servant."

"Then I shall put myself in your competent hands. They have proved more than adequate in the past." After a pause, he added in a quieter voice, "I don't know if I have thanked you sufficiently for that."

She glanced up at him as if looking for sarcasm. Finding none, she continued to look at him. "I was very concerned about you at the time," she said honestly. "You had an ugly cut in your head. Did it heal completely?"

"I have only a slight scar but my hair covers it." The carriage swayed, and he tightened his hold around her. He didn't release it even when they were rolling along smoothly again.

He was alone with her now. It would be the ideal opportunity to ask questions about Frederick. Yet he found himself reluctant to bring up the subject. He and Cornelia were finally relaxed with each other, and he did not want to destroy the mood between them. So they rode along in companionable silence until they reached the Halsey's.

There he handed her out of the carriage, and they walked in the back door. Cornelia was shown up a narrow rear staircase to the third floor servants' quarters. Edwin sat down in the kitchen on a rough-hewn bench in front of a large fireplace.

It was a novel experience for Lord Taveston to sit by the fire while a maid peeled potatoes across from him. Edwin Sorrels had often been in these situations, but never Lord Taveston.

Had the Halseys known he was here, he was certain they would have rushed downstairs and urged him into their best parlor. If it was unusual for a peer to sit in the Halsey's kitchen, it was equally so for Lady Devenish to be upstairs tending to sick servants, he reflected.

Stretching out his legs, Edwin examined the tassels on his Hessians and tried to name another lady he knew who would do what Cornelia was doing. Lady Mittenhoff might have in her day. She had once smuggled documents out of Russia in the not insubstantial bosom of her gown. But she was elderly now and confined to sitting in her rooms and receiving callers. Then there was Rowena Cavendish who had made rooms available to poverty-stricken women living on the streets of London.

He admired those two women because they had not let their place in society keep them from helping others. He believed wealth and privilege brought with it social responsibilities. He had a tremendous admiration for the women who used their position to help others.

The door opened and a head appeared briefly. "You going to be all day peeling those potatoes, girl? Hurry up or I'll turn you off without a reference."

The scolding clearly unsettled the girl. He watched as she tried to peel faster and ended up slicing into her finger.

"Oh!" Tears came into her eyes.

"Here. Let me help."

Edwin was peeling potatoes by the time Cornelia returned back downstairs. She paused and looked at him, then burst out laughing.

"Careful, my dear, you would not want to anger a man who is holding a knife." He held up the paring knife and a peeling slid off it.

She tried to hide her laughter behind her hands. He had never noticed before how beautiful her hands were. They were strong and capable looking with lovely long fingers. She looked impish and appealing peeping out from behind them.

Edwin rose and offered his arm with exaggerated courtliness. "May I escort you out to the carriage, my dear?"

Cornelia was still giggling as she put her fingers over his arm. She turned her face up to his, and he saw the laughter sparkling in her eyes. Some of London's most beautiful women had clung to the arm she touched, but he had seldom felt as oddly anxious for the moment to continue as he did now.

Outside, he handed her in, got in after her and pulled the door closed.

She relaxed back against the squabs and closed her eyes.

"Tired?" he asked.

"A bit." She opened her eyes. "Thank you for coming with me. I often wished Frederick had accompanied me when I was called out, but he never did. When I am with a sick person, it's nice to know someone is waiting for me."

He sat back beside her. Their shoulders met in a way that seemed comfortable. Neither pulled away.

The urge to touch her cheek was almost as strong as the warning not to. He did not want to ruin the moment by doing anything to make her draw away.

So he contented himself with looking at her and inhaling the scent of lavender that clung to her cloak. He followed the trace of her lashes as she closed them in a blink that was almost sensuous and then opened them again.

"May I ask you a question, milord?"

"Of course you can, Cornelia."

The mischief that came into her brown eyes made them sparkle even more. The urge to touch her rose up strongly; he had to concentrate to stifle it.

"If my kitchen maid is ever ill, will you come over and peel potatoes for me?"

"It depends on the persuasion offered," he drawled.

That brought a momentary blush to her cheeks but she rallied quickly. "I don't know what sort of inducement you are usually offered, milord, but I can promise all the potatoes you can eat."

He smiled at her.

As much as he enjoyed the flirtation between them, he could not let this opportunity to probe for information pass.

"Cornelia, at the risk of destroying the good will between us, I must ask you some questions. Please don't refuse to answer."

He saw caution come into her face, but she did not move away from him. "It's about Frederick, isn't it?"

"Yes."

She folded her hands in her lap and sat waiting, like a child about to endure something unpleasant. It was still painful for her to talk about Frederick, he realized.

"You know your husband was shot for a reason. It might help me discover who killed him if you tell me something about his activities the days before he died."

Silence. For a moment he feared that she would not answer. Then she began to speak softly, pausing now and then to search for words.

"His last days were like any other. He consulted with the overseer, went into town occasionally, met with the vicar and the local squire and his friends. Those are the ordinary sorts of things men in his position do. At least," she continued in a barely audible voice, "that is what he told me at the time that he was doing. I do not know what he really did."

She looked lost and close to tears. He believed she had indeed told him all she knew, and he did not press further.

The carriage pulled to a halt, and they were back at her house.

"The game is called Charades," the petite Lady Hauserman explained from the front of her overdecorated pink salon.

Margaret had stayed home this evening complaining of weariness. Lord Bettonbrook had sent Cornelia a note saying that he would not be attending either. She had been grateful to hear from him. After seeing his displeasure over Lord Taveston's gift, she had feared he might not continue calling on her.

The room she was sitting in was hot from a blazing fire and a barrage of flaming candelabras. Poor old Lord Kilmer looked as if he were about to expire from the heat. Small wonder Lord Hauserman chose not to attend his wife's soiree, Cornelia reflected.

"I believe that Charades was invented in France," Lady Hauserman said.

Of course, Cornelia thought with a wry smile. Everything of fashion came from there. How ironic that even the waistlines of women's gowns were in the French Empire style when England was at war with that country. Every household with any pretense to respectability employed a French chef, the more temperamental the better. Most families boasted a French governess who said her family was of old and established nobility and had barely escaped the guillotine.

"It is played by acting out the words of books or plays. You are not allowed to speak." Lady Hauserman smiled around the room at the two dozen or so people sitting on her pink Louis XIV chairs. She pressed her hands together girlishly. "We shall have ever so much fun. Who shall be first?"

The bemused guests regarded her in silence.

"Come, come, let us not be bashful." Lady Hauserman waved a delicate hand. "Ah, Lord Taveston, I see you trying to hide behind Mrs. Trundle's hat. Pray why don't you begin?"

Beside Cornelia, Anne Wallace murmured, "He is too concerned with whether he will spoil the folds of his cravat to be good at this sort of game."

Cornelia turned to her companion. She and Anne had gone to Miss Burton's School for Young Ladies together. "Do you know Lord Taveston?" She tried not to sound too curious.

"Of course."

As a newcomer to London, Cornelia had been careful not to ask many questions about the earl. One never knew who was connected to whom. Quite aside from that, Cornelia could scarcely go about fashionable London inquiring about a gentleman, especially when she was being courted by another man. "How do you know him?" Cornelia asked casually.

"My dear, everyone knows the Earl of Taveston. His family is wealthy and influential. He and my brother went to Eton together."

"Eton," Cornelia repeated. Frederick had gone there. She looked toward the front of the room where Lord Taveston stood holding up three fingers. Frederick and Lord Taveston were about the same age; they must have known each other as schoolboys.

"It's a play with three words," Lady Hauserman explained.

The earl nodded. He looked elaborately groomed in white unmentionables and a slate blue jacket. The quizzing glass was out of sight for the moment, but he looked every inch the dandy as he smiled at the audience with easy, bored charm.

Watching him now, it was easy for Cornelia to believe he had been an Eton man. But the man she had met last summer—the one who had shown little polish and yet whom she had found strangely appealing—who was he and how did he fit into the mystery that was Lord Taveston? The man who had escorted her to the Halsey's mansion and waited while she tended a sick servant, was he the real Earl of Taveston? She had certainly felt a greater warmth toward him after that journey.

Anne leaned toward her. "I have heard Lord Taveston bought you a gift. Have a care you don't fall top over tail in love with him. He can be dreadfully shallow and cavalier. This Season he seems particularly so. He worries more about the cut of his coat than anything else." The other woman sighed. "A pity. He was not always so lacking in substance. When he was younger, he was very concerned with the state of the world. 'Tis a shame he has changed so."

"Yes." What would Anne say if she knew Lord Taveston was working for his country in ways that must often be dangerous? Cornelia's thoughts moved to another man who had helped his country. Frederick had paid for his patriotism with his life. Why hadn't Frederick trusted her enough to tell her what he was doing? How could she ever trust another man after her husband had so betrayed her love for him?

"The Beggar's Opera!" someone near her guessed.

She looked up, her attention called back to the game. People in the audience were animated as they called out suggestions to the name of the play.

At the front of the room, Lord Taveston took an imaginary woman into his arms, dipped her until she was half reclining and looked passionately down at her.

Cornelia thought of how snugly his arm had fit around her shoulder in his carriage and how near they had sat to each other.

Lord Taveston kissed the make-believe woman.

She imagined herself in his arms with his lips hovering inches above hers. Her mouth dried to dust.

"The Rake's Progress!"

"The London Cuckold's," came an earthy suggestion from the back of the room.

"Pray let us not be so cynical about love," tiny Lady Hauserman rose to admonish reprovingly.

At the front of the room Lord Taveston looked longingly down at the "woman" in his arms.

"Romeo and Juliet," Cornelia heard herself say.

The earl raised his head. "Lady Devenish has guessed the answer."

Several people clapped. Cornelia blushed not because of the attention but because Lord Taveston continued to look steadily at her. Her thoughts felt transparent; she was certain he could read them even from across the room. He must know she had foolishly imagined him kissing her. Her blush deepened.

Lady Hauserman hurried to the front of the room. "Splendidly done, Lord Taveston. Let us have another volunteer, please."

"That was a very good guess," Anne leaned over to say to her.

"Thank you."

The room probably was not as hot as it suddenly seemed, but Cornelia was unable to remain in it. Quietly she slipped from her chair and out into the hall. Her footsteps were silenced by the thick Aubusson carpet. As she walked the length of the hallway, she tried to forget the look that had passed between her and Lord Taveston.

Pausing at the end of the corridor, she gazed out the window that overlooked the side of the house where the carriages were parked. Torches punctuated the darkness and provided enough light so she could see horses eating from oat bags. Under a beam of light, several drivers engaged in a game of dice on the road. She was starting to turn away when a movement off in the corner caught her eye. She looked back. Dimly she could distinguish two men facing each other in the shadows of the neigh-

114

boring house. The shorter of the two men handed something to the taller, who then crept away around the side of the Hauserman house.

Odd, she thought. She was certain the taller man was wearing an opera hat. But that would imply he was a man of station, and what would a man of station be doing lurking about in the shadows with the servants?

Cornelia was curious enough to push through the door into the dark library. The door swung closed behind her as she crossed the long room to the bay window. There she peered out to try to see the direction the man in the opera hat had taken. Perhaps if she saw him closer she would recognize him.

Her sarcenet gown with black silk underslip rustled as she bent toward the window. The sound was loud in the empty room. The only other noise was that of a clock ticking. And of someone breathing.

Cornelia froze. Someone breathing?

Whoever it was was standing very close to her. Behind the draperies? The room was so dark the person could be anywhere, even close enough to reach out and touch her.

The thought of a clammy hand touching her arm was all her overworked imagination needed to propel her into action.

Whirling, she fled. As she ran the length of the room, her skirts crashed with the volume of cymbals. She pushed through the door, rushed into the hallway, and ran straight into Lord Taveston. Instinctively he put out his hands to keep her from falling. She shrank away from him.

"What's wrong?" he demanded.

"There's someone in there," Cornelia said breathlessly. "Someone is st-standing in the dark."

She pointed back into the room with a shaking hand.

He looked from the door back to her. "You were in there alone in the dark?"

"Yes, I—Yes." She left it at that. She was too perturbed to explain she had gone into the room hoping to glimpse the mysterious man in the opera hat through the window.

The earl plucked a taper from a hall sconce and stepped into the room. Cornelia followed cautiously. He used the taper to light several candles in a candelabra. She stayed close beside him as he looked behind the draperies and the sofas.

The room was empty.

He turned to her. "I thought you said there was someone in here."

"There was. I heard him breathing."

"It might have been your own breathing you heard," he said reasonably.

"It was not mine. It was someone else's." Her nerves were jangled and his doubt only increased her agitation. Glancing around the room, she saw a door. "He may have left through there."

The earl walked over and tried the handle. "No one left through here. It is locked."

During the silence that followed, he studied her closely. The candelabra cast a large shadow of him on the wall behind him. The shadow loomed large and ominous. "Pray forgive my curiosity, but what were you doing in a pitch dark room while a party was in progress down the hall?"

"I wanted a breath of air. It had become unbearably hot in the room."

"It is indeed warm down there, but surely you

need not have come all the way down the hall to an unlit room?"

It was a reasonable question. She looked away.

"Were you meeting someone?"

"Of course not."

"You needn't look so indignant, Cornelia. It is perfectly natural for a woman to be so charmed by a man that she allows him to persuade her to meet him privately. However, you should be warned that some men are less, ah, trustworthy than others."

"I am not a naive child," she said frostily.

"Of course not. But neither are you used to the ways of London men," he pointed out. "I am only trying to offer advice."

She remained rigid. "I am perfectly capable of taking care of myself." She might not have all the polish of Lady Jane, but she was not an idiot. "If you will excuse me, I shall return to the others."

"Of course," he said with light sarcasm. "Allow me to escort you back."

Cornelia placed a stiff hand over the arm he offered and walked out of the room and down the hall with him. Neither spoke.

A few late guests were still arriving, but she was too indignant to even nod to balding Sir Adam or smile at the flustered Stillmans as Lady Stillman patted at her hair before entering the salon.

How insulting of Lord Taveston to suggest she would make assignations to meet strange men in deserted rooms. Just because she had lived all her life in the country did not mean she was naive.

Several pairs of eyes glanced up with undisguised curiosity as she and Lord Taveston entered the room together. The Hornaby sisters nudged

117

each other. Cornelia pretended not to notice as she sat down beside Anne and picked up her fan again.

The game of Charades was still in progress.

Lord Taveston sat down beside her. He took up his quizzing glass and inspected his jacket for traces of lint. Once again he was the perfect dandy.

"Two words," Lady Hauserman announced while a heavy gentleman stood beside her holding up two fingers. The man then put his index finger in front of his lips in a shushing gesture.

"Where were you?" Anne leaned over to ask Cornelia. "I was beginning to worry."

"A Secret Assignation," Lord Taveston said.

Cornelia turned a dark look on him. "I did *not* go there for an assignation."

"I was guessing the name of the play," he said innocently.

Fuming, Cornelia turned away. Why couldn't the man sit elsewhere? How could she possibly concentrate on Charades now?

"Mrs. Summerfield has guessed it. It is *Whispered Confidences*!" Lady Hauserman enthused from the front of the room.

Cornelia prayed for the evening to end or at least for Lord Taveston to move away. She wondered how she could have felt so comfortable with him only yesterday. Now she felt tense and uncharitable toward him.

How was it that every time she met the man he stirred up emotions of one sort or another? She was able to see Lord Bettonbrook time after time, and there was scarcely a ripple of emotion between them. Yet every time she came into contact with the earl, there was an incident of magnitude between them. Either he was making her like him more by putting her at ease as he had in the carriage, or he was making her like him less by being as insulting as he had been this evening. Nothing remained on an even keel with him long.

Chapter 8

The next morning Cornelia and Elizabeth were ready to go out for a walk when Lord Bettonbrook called. She was glad to see him after the strained way his visit had ended the other day. He brought a nosegay of primroses and a sweet doll dressed in blue satin for Elizabeth.

Cornelia picked up her daughter and held her so that she could see the present. "Look what Lord Bettonbrook has given you, pet. You must thank him."

The little girl clutched at the doll. Then she reached up and gave Lord Bettonbrook a messy but heartfelt kiss. He looked startled. Clearly his lordship was not used to children's kisses.

The marquis cleared his throat with grave dignity. "I wish to apologize for any ill-advised comments I made when last I saw you. Naturally you are at liberty to accept gifts from anyone you please."

"It was not precisely a gift," she insisted. It was more in the way of payment for a favor I had done Lord Taveston. Pray do not consider the matter further." He looked doubtful but willing to be reassured. She tried for a change of subject. "Elizabeth and I were about to go for a walk. Would you like to accompany us?"

He hesitated.

She smiled. "I promise she won't kiss you again."

He smiled wanly. "It is not that I object to children, you know. It is simply that I am not accustomed to them."

"I understand." Lord Bettonbrook was kind with Elizabeth, but he was awkward with her. Cornelia suspected he would be that way with his own children if he were ever to have any. There were worse things than a man being ill at ease with the young, she told herself. Plenty of men ignored their offspring altogether and only saw them for a few moments each day while a nanny hovered nearby. That was not the life Cornelia wanted for her children, and Elizabeth must be taken into consideration when she thought of remarriage.

Lord Bettonbrook made up his mind. "Yes, I should be glad to walk with you."

Cornelia carried Elizabeth down the front steps and put her down. The little girl toddled ahead.

"A fine day," Lord Bettonbrook commented with a look upward at the sky.

"It is." Being with him felt comfortable. She knew that he would stay with safe topics like the weather. There was none of the unpredictability she felt when she was around Lord Taveston. Certainly Lord Bettonbrook would not mention Frederick or awaken conflicting emotions inside her about how she felt toward her dead husband.

"Did you enjoy Lady Hauserman's soiree?" he inquired.

"Yes. We played a game called Charades."

He shuddered. "I am glad I was not present. I detest parlor games."

"It was not so bad," she objected mildly. Had she not been preoccupied with Lord Taveston and the incident in the library, she could have even enjoyed the game more.

Ahead of them, Elizabeth tumbled to the ground and paused to determine if she wished to cry before pushing herself up to pursue a butterfly.

Lord Bettonbrook and Cornelia walked behind at a leisurely pace.

"I was at White's earlier," he said. "News of the war is grim. Napoleon is said to be building strength across the channel."

She searched his face anxiously. "Do you fear an invasion?"

"There has been talk of an invasion for some time," Bettonbrook said solemnly. "But there has never been such a concentration of men and materials before. I believe the French may indeed be preparing to storm our shores this time."

The thought chilled Cornelia. "Will we be prepared if that happens?"

"I hope so." He assisted her over a broken spot in the cobblestone sidewalk, then continued, "The French have a better network of spies than we. They seem to know our every move."

Cornelia was silent as she thought about Frederick and the part he had played in spying. It had ultimately cost him his life.

"Don't look so worried, my dear. I did not mean to upset you. I'm sure our shores are perfectly safe, and certainly you needn't worry about spies. You and I are scarcely likely to come into contact with them."

"Of course not," she murmured and thought of Lord Taveston. Was he safe? Someone could lie in wait for him as they had for Frederick, she realized, and felt something tighten inside her.

When next she spoke with him, she must caution him to take care, especially now that the situation between England and France was worse. As Frederick's widow, she owed that much to the Cause.

"I should not have said anything," Lord Bettonbrook said. "Now you are silent and frightened."

She could not tell him her true thoughts. Already he seemed to harbor some jealousy toward the earl, and she was not going to make that worse by introducing Lord Taveston's name.

They had circled the block and were back at her house. Cornelia invited him in for tea. Elizabeth was sent up to the nursery and Cornelia and the marquis sat down and had a quiet conversation over tea and scones.

Their talk was not lively or full of coy glances, but she was too mature to expect such girlish things. They had a very sensible talk and parted feeling very amiable toward each other.

Cornelia had just finished treating a housemaid's headache with cured grains of paradise when Robert appeared at the door. Robert worked at her stables. He was a large man with slow speech but a ready smile.

"I've the fever, ma'am." He sat down on the wooden bench at the small table, put his elbows on the table, and looked plaintively up at her.

She touched his flushed brow. "You have indeed. How long have you been ill, Robert?"

"Started night before last."

"Have you taken anything for it?" she asked as she began to search in her bag.

"Chewed some turnip roots."

"We shall try a tea from leaves of the sourwood and see if that cures you."

He nodded and spread his large hands out on the table to wait.

Cornelia tied an apron around her and began moving briskly about the kitchen putting water on to boil and reaching past a cook's helper for a mortar and pestle. The servants had grown so accustomed to seeing her in here in the mornings that they paid her little attention.

"I should not have been up in the middle of the night," Robert said mournfully. "Not when it was raining and the air so damp."

"No, you should not have," she agreed. "You must be more careful about your health."

"Ay, but the horse needed seeing to. I could not leave it standing in the stall dripping wet."

Cornelia lifted the kettle of boiling water from the stove and frowned. "Why was the horse wet? Does the stable leak?"

"No, ma'am. It's a good tight stable, that it is. Fine roof. No, there's no leak, but someone took the horse out after I went to bed. Didn't bring the poor creature back 'til 'round one or so in the morning."

She stared at him, the tea kettle forgotten in her hand. "Why would anyone take a horse out at that hour?"

"Don't know. Heard the stable door closin' and climbed down to look. That's when I found the mare all cold and dripping. She had been ridden hard."

"When did this happen?" Cornelia didn't even

notice the steam rising from the kettle she still held and floating in front of her face.

"Couple of nights ago."

"Why was I not informed?"

He shrugged. "Didn't want to raise a fuss and worry you." Rising, he took the kettle from her and poured water into the cup containing the leaves of sourwood.

Cornelia watched him with pursed lips. Frederick would have been told if he had been alive. She was on the verge of saying as much when she guiltily reminded herself that Frederick had spent more time at the stables and had displayed a greater interest in its concerns than she. Still, she could not let this event pass unremarked.

"I cannot have my servants going about in London in the middle of the night," she said sternly. "If an incident like this happens again, you are to notify me."

He nodded and meekly drank the tea.

She continued to mull over who might have gone out at that hour. A maid on some tryst? Surely a maid would not have ridden through the night streets of London alone. A male servant headed for the gaming dens or cockfights? That was possible. But taking a horse from the stables was daring, and she could not imagine a servant doing it merely for a game. That meant the mission might have been more serious. Was someone in trouble?

She had eleven household servants here in London, and there was Robert and Jack in the stables. She thought about each one in turn and tried to recall if she had noted anyone acting suspiciously of late.

She was thus engaged when a maid arrived with

a message that the nanny and Elizabeth awaited her in the hall.

"Dear me, is it time already?" She had plans to take her daughter out today and had instructed the nanny to have her ready at eleven. Cornelia hurried out of the kitchen, untying her muslin apron as she went.

In the front hall, little Elizabeth was all smiles and eagerness. She held out her hands to Cornelia. "Uut," she said.

"Yes, 'out'. Mama is going to take you to Burlington Arcade so that you can look in the windows at all the pretty things."

"Uut!"

"But you shall be the prettiest thing in all of Burlington Arcade," Cornelia informed her with a mother's pardonable pride.

The carriage ride over was pleasant if hectic. Elizabeth bounced from window to window to look out. The matronly, cheerful nanny tried without success to restrain her.

Once they reached the Arcade with its row of covered shops, each with a bow window displaying its wares, Elizabeth distinguished herself by pointing at a lady in a dress the color of green pond scum and shrieking "Bad, bad dress!" She later planted herself in front of a chocolate shop and tried to reach through the glass for a piece. Her failure to grasp the candy brought on a fit of crying.

"There, there, sweetheart. Let Mama hold you."

Elizabeth was thus weeping against her mother's shoulder when Lord Taveston exited from a tailor's shop nearby. Cornelia noted absently that he scarcely looked like a man in need of a tailor. He was already perfectly dressed in a gray jacket, tan waistcoat, and pair of charcoal trousers. A gold watch fob dangled near his watch pocket and a monocle showed in his breastpocket.

He paused when he saw them and executed a bow.

"Good morning, Lord Taveston," Cornelia said. Elizabeth continued to sob against her.

The earl returned her greeting but his gaze was on Elizabeth. "Your daughter seems unhappy."

"There was a matter of some c-a-n-d-y," Cornelia explained in careful spelling.

"Ah." He nodded heavily. "I apprehend she enjoys such morsels?"

Cornelia smiled. "All too dearly."

Elizabeth, realizing she was the subject of their conversation, emerged from her tears and her mother's shoulder to look at the visitor.

Lord Taveston addressed himself to her. "Perhaps you would permit me to take you and your mother for an ice at Gunthers, my dear."

Elizabeth had had an ice only once in her young life, but the memory remained vivid. She burst into a smile and thrust her hands toward the earl.

"Darling, I am persuaded that Lord Taveston does not wish to hold you—"

He took Elizabeth from her arms and held her with the ease of experience. "Three nieces and two nephews," he explained over the little girl's head. "Do I have your permission to escort you and your party to Gunthers, Lady Devenish?"

"It's hardly a fair question now, my lord. My daughter will never forgive me if she does not get to go."

He grinned. "Having to deal with men who try

to charm your daughter is one of the trials of motherhood."

It was she who felt charmed at the moment, Cornelia thought dazedly. It was hard not to like the man when he was holding her only child. Elizabeth tipped his hat off and he caught it by the rim as it fell. His foppish manners had vanished, and he was once again the man she had known last summer. His engaging smile disarmed her as they set off for Gunthers. Any unpleasant thoughts of him at Lady Hauserman's were forgotten.

Settled in his arms, Elizabeth tugged at his cravat. Cornelia reached for the busy little hands. "You must not do that, pet." But it was already too late.

Cornelia bit her lip. "Oh, dear." She looked regretfully up at Lord Taveston. "I'm sorry, milord, but I'm afraid she has ruined your cravat." She held out her hands to take her daughter back.

Elizabeth clung to the earl, and he continued to hold her calmly. "What's this you say? The little minx has ruined my cravat? My valet will have her head." That warning was accompanied by a tickle that sent Elizabeth into peals of giggles.

Any lingering resistance toward the earl melted away. Her good feelings toward him rose higher as they partook of ices at Gunthers. She was even more endeared to him when he continued to hold Elizabeth after she was sticky with chocolate.

He told a nonsense story to the little girl about elves and tiny horses. He considerately included the nanny in the conversation, and it was very shortly plain that that good woman was smittened with him.

Cornelia was having such a pleasant time, she

was disappointed when the earl finally took them back to their carriage. While the nanny settled Elizabeth inside, Cornelia lingered at the door and smiled at him. "Thank you for a most enjoyable afternoon, milord."

He inclined his head. There were chocolate smudges on his snow-white cravat. "No doubt I shall see you this evening at the Wilsons."

"Perhaps."

Cornelia had considered staying home tonight and resting, but now she decided that she would go to the Wilsons. She was not going solely because Lord Taveston would be there. Well . . . perhaps she was. But there was nothing wrong in feeling agreeable toward him, she told herself. He had known her husband, and it would not be untoward for her to be friends with him.

If some niggling doubts about his motives for being so nice to her today crept into her mind, she ignored them. She also pushed aside thoughts of how Lord Bettonbrook would react if she were to develop a friendship with the Earl of Taveston.

She had barely entered the house when Margaret whisked down the steps in a swirl of skirts. She held aloft an envelope. "I have had a letter from my brother, and he is coming to visit!"

Cornelia looked at Margaret's radiant face and felt a stab of guilt that she had not realized how much her friend missed her brother. Judging from Margaret's smile, however, she had indeed been lonely for her brother.

"I hope it is all right for him to stay here?" Margaret said. "The house is quite spacious. I didn't see any problem with it."

"It is fine for him to stay." Since he was a vicar,

there was little danger of gossip. Besides, Margaret was an eminently proper chaperon. "When will he arrive?"

"Tomorrow. Isn't it by everything wonderful!"

"Yes." If the vicar was arriving tomorrow, he must already be en route. Wheels turned in the back of her mind. "You asked him to come, didn't you?"

Margaret flushed and lowered her eyes. "Yes. I'm sorry. I should not have done so without consulting you."

"It's perfectly all right." It was Cornelia who felt regretful. She should have realized how lonely Margaret was for Walter.

"I'm glad he's coming, Margaret." She meant to go out of her way to make him welcome.

Lord Taveston circulated around the party slowly while Lady Jane clung to his side and laughed up at him. She was a wonderful diversion. With her beside him, men noticed her rather than him. That was exactly what he wanted. He must be able to scrutinize the crowd without attracting undue attention.

It helped enormously that Lady Jane had friends in the highest places. He had learned some interesting tidbits from her—like the fact a certain duke had gone to Dover this week and that a lady he knew was rumored to be in contact with a French diplomat.

He was anxious to discuss all this with Linton. The young viscount was to have returned from Paris yesterday and was to be here tonight to pass along the information he had gleaned there. The hour was growing late. Why wasn't he here?

Perhaps the viscount was in another room. He would circulate a bit and surely find him. When Lady Jane went off to dance, he headed down the hall to the gaming room.

The tables in the crowded green salon were full of players of both sexes. Spectators stood sipping sherry and taking bets on who would win.

From the corner of the room, Lord Bettonbrook hailed him. "Care to join us in a rubber of whist, Taveston?"

It was a tame game, but he sat down and took up a hand. Perhaps Linton would show up later.

The young buck beside the earl was deep in his cups and liquor had made his tongue loose. "I say, Bettonbrook," he slurred, "the betting at White's is five to one that you are going to offer for Sir Frederick's widow before the week is out."

Lord Bettonbrook placed a card carefully and mutely sorted through those remaining in his hand.

"D'ya hear me, Bettonbrook?"

"I would not deign to dignify such an impertinent question," he said stiffly.

"Give over, Bettonbrook. D'ya mean to get yourself leg shackled or not? I've got a quid riding on it."

"Then you shall have to take your chances, won't you?"

Lord Taveston glanced toward the older man. *Was* Bettonbrook going to offer? And if he did, would Cornelia accept? She was young enough to be his daughter. She should marry someone closer to her own age and someone not as stuffy as the marquis. Frederick had not been stuffy, Edwin reflected.

It annoyed him to think of Cornelia wasting herself on the marquis. She ought to have more sense.

"Your turn, Taveston."

He laid a card and promptly lost it. He had grown good at losing at cards. To win would display more shrewdness than he wanted to reveal, but if he were to play for real he'd wager he would win every hand. However, impressing people was not his object. Getting them not to take him seriously was his goal. It seemed to work well, he reflected as he slid a glance toward the doorway. Where the devil was Linton?

The card game continued. People came to watch over his shoulder. "I see you're still losing, Taveston."

"Merely a bad hand. My luck will change momentarily," he said with supercilious confidence.

"They're all bad hands for you. You should give up playing."

Edwin ignored that.

Others came to watch, than wandered off. He felt someone slip a note into his pocket, but he didn't acknowledge the gesture by so much as a blink. He continued to pick out bad cards and lay them down.

At length he rose. "My luck is off a bit this evening. I am persuaded I will be in better form when I play again."

"Stay for another hand, Taveston. You're getting better at the game. Honestly you are."

"You just want the blunt you can win from him, Wickley."

Edwin rose and made elaborate work of straightening his coat. "I must attend to the lovely Lady Jane." With an overdone, flourishing bow, he exited the room.

He was almost consumed with impatience to read the note, but he dare not do that here. Instead he went in search of Lady Jane and found her talking with Cornelia and Margaret.

Cornelia glanced up as Lord Taveston sat down beside Lady Jane. She felt dull next to Lady Jane's glittering beauty. At the moment the other woman was telling about her visit to Sussex.

"Visiting the Willoughbys is always so civilized," Lady Jane said. "They are some of the few people who know how to give a party. Their parties are not boring stale-cake-and-warm-punch affairs."

Cornelia would never be invited to the rarefied houseparties given by the Willoughbys. Although she was of good birth, certain doors were closed to her. All doors were open to Lady Jane, she acknowledged with a touch of envy. She looked at the way Lord Taveston sat so close to the other woman and felt an even deeper envy.

"I'm so glad the Willoughbys are back in London and are having a party next week," Lady Jane continued. "All the best people will be there."

Cornelia had not been invited.

"There you are, my dear." Lady Jane turned her attention to Lord Taveston. Seeing the pair smiling with such burning intensity at each other made something in Cornelia's throat tighten. She slipped off to join Margaret in the next room.

"Stand in front of me, Cornelia, so that Lady Jane doesn't see me eating stale cake and drinking warm punch."

Cornelia smiled wanly.

"Whatever does Taveston see in her?" Margaret asked between mouthfuls.

"She is young and beautiful. She has a lovely figure. She is from one of the best families, and she has money." Listing the other woman's assets depressed her even more. "Small wonder he finds her attractive."

"She lets him know of her attraction to him. I think you are not disinterested in him. You should make your feelings known to him."

Cornelia made a wry face. "I could scarcely compete with her even if I wanted to." She glanced over her shoulder and saw Lady Jane bending to whisper something in the earl's ear. Cornelia looked away, fighting down a hollow feeling. "I have no interest in Lord Taveston anyway."

Margaret raised her eyebrows.

"Nor has he in me," she added.

"One never knows about men," Margaret said mysteriously. "They can surprise you."

"Have you been surprised?" Cornelia asked more to distract herself than from any curiosity.

"I indulged in some light flirtations when I was young," Margaret said. She laughed sadly, "However, now that I am nine and twenty, I am too old to attract a man. I have been too long on the shelf."

"There are older men," Cornelia objected. But she knew Margaret had little dowry and the chances of her catching a man's attention were, quite honestly, small.

"I am not complaining," Margaret said. "I find being hostess to my brother fulfilling enough."

"Yes, I am sure it is very rewarding." In truth, Cornelia could not imagine anything duller than spending every day in the little vicarage in the company of Walter. He was a very good man, but boring. Margaret was capable of laughter and good spirits even if she did sometimes show a moodier side of herself. Walter seemed not to possess the ability for gaity.

Cornelia's gaze went back to Lady Jane and the earl.

Chapter 9

"Come to me tonight, my angel," the note read. It was written in a curling hand and embellished with a heart. As soon as he had deposited Lady Jane at her doorstep, Edwin rushed to the small house on Juniper Street in his gaudy crimson carriage.

The buxom, red-haired woman who answered the door greeted him with a kiss and drew him inside. The rooms were decorated in rose and cream and looked like the courtesan's nest that they were. He knew he could leave his carriage out front without fear anyone would discover his true mission. Any man who was seen entering Melinda's house was thought to be here to sample her favors.

He bent to kiss her neck. "Where is Linton?" he whispered.

She laughed lustily. "Later, my love. There will be time for all that and more. First you must have something to drink. Come into the salon."

A stiff-lipped servant hovering nearby disappeared and reappeared a few moments later in the salon with port and stem glasses. The earl sipped at the port. It was not difficult for him to play the part of a man desperate to go upstairs to her rooms. He did indeed want to be alone with her, but not for the obvious reason.

After they finished their drinks, she led him up the steps. Her giggles and whispered promises could be heard by anyone caring to listen.

Once inside her bedroom, she closed the door and locked it. Her brassy smile faded. Now she was all seriousness. "He's in here," she said in a low voice.

"Is he hurt?"

"No."

She led Edwin to a small dressing room and closed and locked that door. Linton appeared from behind a mirror. His unruly reddish hair and freckled face made him appear younger than his twenty years. Only those who looked closer would note that his innocent-looking eyes belied a keen intelligence. He had been in and out of France under a thousand disguises. He was one of the best operators England had. For him to be hiding here meant something was very wrong.

"What happened?" Edwin demanded.

"Someone tried to kill me on my way back from Dover last night," he said tersely.

"How did you escape?"

"By slipping off my horse in the high grass and crawling into the woods. Whoever was after me thought I was riding low in the saddle, so he kept pursuing the stallion."

Edwin nodded his approval. "Good thinking. Where were you set upon?"

"I was on a sideroad where no highwayman would wait."

"How many men attacked you?"

"Only one."

The two exchanged glances.

"That's exactly what happened to Frederick," Edwin said.

"I have been thinking that very thing. The French have ears in high places or they never would have known what road I was on."

"They do indeed have some powerful sources." Wearily, he thought of the last six weeks he had spent attending every tiresome society event and watching for any suspicious actions. He had not yet discovered anything concrete although he was forming some suspicions.

"Have you been able to learn anything of value from Lady Devenish?" Linton asked.

"No." He paused, then continued, "One night I did find her leaving the library at the Hauserman's house. She said someone was in the library in the dark, but when I checked the room was empty."

Linton looked grim. "Lord Hauserman is in the War Department and privy to some highly secret information. Someone could have been looking for that information."

"Perhaps."

"Where is Linton to go now?" Melinda interrupted to ask. "He cannot stay here much longer without the servants becoming suspicious."

"I'll send a coach for him later tonight. He can climb out your window." Edwin smiled. "I daresay it won't be the first time a man has gone out through your window."

She gave a saucy toss of her head. "As a rule they are climbing *in*."

He chuckled.

Linton remained serious. "Have you any thoughts who the man in the library might have been?"

"No. But now that Spain has joined forces with France and declared war on England, Napoleon's naval superiority will be established and our fleet outnumbered. It is more important than ever that we uncover the traitors."

"Yes, and we must use anyone to that end."

Lord Taveston nodded.

Once he was back in his carriage, he concentrated on the problem. He passed through Mayfair on his way home and glanced out at the house Cornelia had taken. His thoughts strayed from business to personal. Cornelia was doubtless inside singing to her child or preparing for bed. The warm, family scene he evoked for himself of a woman and her child made him slightly wistful. In the past he had spent little time yearning for domestic life, but lately he found the notion of a woman waiting for him each night growing in appeal. Thoughts of gentle hands and soft murmurings kept creeping into his mind at the most unexpected times.

Perhaps next Season he would look at the crop of debutantes and think about a wife, he told himself. Now, back to matters of importance like spies and traitors.

The next evening Cornelia stood in her bedroom in her chemise while her maid held up a gray gown in one hand a brown in the other. "Which do you wish to wear this evening?"

Cornelia looked at the bland colors and thought of Lady Jane's pretty gowns. Rebellion stirred. "Neither," she said firmly. "What has become of my blue frock? I have not worn it since before Elizabeth's birth, but I believe it will fit me still."

Beth blinked. "The blue gown, milady?"

"Yes." The dress in question was cut low enough to reveal an expanse of bosom Cornelia usually kept modestly covered. Added to that, there was something almost sensuous about the way the dress moved. It flowed in ripples below her knees. Above the knees it clung in ways that outlined thighs and, yes, milady's derrier.

The maid helped Cornelia into the gown, then stood back wordlessly.

Cornelia looked at the way the gown accented each feminine curve and began to lose confidence. She bit her lower lip. "Is it too revealing?"

"No, ma'am. You look beautiful. The grays and the browns never made you look as pretty as you do now."

Cornelia turned to face the cheval glass. The blue was a pleasant compliment to the pink on her cheekbones and the paleness of her skin, she admitted.

Her gaze went to her hair. The prim bun was a matronly style. While she certainly was not trying to look like a green girl, it would not hurt for her to have a style that was a bit more à la mode.

She pushed her fingers through her hair, fluffing it up in front. That wasn't so bad. There was no reason she could not keep the bun in back and have the front hair cut in a shorter, more stylish way.

"Beth, get the scissors."

By the time the maid was through, locks of Cornelia's brown hair lay on the floor and a pretty bunch of small curls framed her face. A blue satin band was threaded through them.

Cornelia blinked at her reflection and murmured, "It scarcely looks like me."

"It's very becoming," Beth assured her.

Cornelia picked up her fan and started out into the hall. There she met Margaret.

"You look splendid," the other woman told her with blunt approval. "I am glad that you have finally had the good sense to realize you must be a bit more daring in your clothes and hair if you mean to bring Bettonbrook up to scratch."

"I am not dressed this way in order to wring a proposal out of Lord Bettonbrook." The precise reasons she had chosen to be more adventuresome in her appearance were not even clear to her, but she was certain they had nothing to do with the marquis.

"If you're not, you ought to be," Margaret replied tartly. "The Season is nearing an end. Soon we will be leaving. If Lord Bettonbrook does not propose soon, you will find yourself sitting back in Devon alone again."

Sitting with Frederick's mother, Cornelia amended silently. She had been having such a good time in London that she had not thought about her return to the estate. If she had a choice, would she accept an offer of marriage rather than return there? No, she would not go that far. Still, it was true she had thought Lord Bettonbrook would offer for her. Margaret was right; the end of the Season was only two weeks away and he had said nothing as yet.

"Is Walter ready?" Cornelia asked. Margaret's

brother had arrived earlier in the day, and they had convinced him to join them this evening.

"I am sure he is. I'll go tap on his door," Margaret said.

By the time they arrived at the ball, Lord Bettonbrook was already there. At the sight of Cornelia, he lifted one eyebrow but said nothing.

"Do you not think Lady Devenish looks very fetching tonight?" Margaret prompted.

"Lady Devenish always looks very presentable." He adjusted his cuffs.

If Lord Bettonbrook was not forthcoming with his compliments, other men were. It was true that younger women continued to claim the lion's share of attention, but Cornelia was asked to dance far more than usual. Her partners also were more openly flirtatious with her, a fact that gave her a secret satisfaction. It was all very well to be the proper widow, but it was fun to act with less restraint now and again.

After a set with an army captain and a quadrille with a man who all but leered at her bare bosom, she stood up with the vicar. They were going down the line in a contradance when she saw Lord Taveston enter the room.

He walked with the bored insouciance he could affect so well. Had this man really peeled potatoes and made her feel warm and comfortable on the carriage ride back from the Halseys? She wondered if he had seen her yet and was immediately annoyed with herself that she should care whether he looked in her direction or not.

"I don't know if I have thanked you for allowing

me to disrupt your household on such short notice," Walter Simpson said.

She glanced back at her partner. "I am glad to have you. And I know Margaret is pleased."

"Yes."

They continued to dance in silence. The vicar was not a man of great conversation, she noted ruefully. As the silence stretched, she was beginning to feel awkward. "I must introduce you to Lord Betton-brook," she said just to have something to talk about. "His aunt lives near where you and Margaret grew up."

Again they were without words. The vicar was a good man but not so easy to talk to. Cornelia was glad when the dance ended.

Lord Taveston seemed to weave in and out of the room. He would appear and ask a woman to dance, then he would step out for a while with the men to smoke a cheroot. Then he would reappear. Cornelia was not without partners, but she kept track of his movements. He must have seen her by now.

Finally the earl was standing by her. He lifted his quizzing glass and surveyed her slowly. His glance took in the blue gown. His eyes did not linger on the bustline but she was certain he noted it.

She resisted the temptation to touch her new curls and smooth them back into place.

He let the quizzing glass dangle and drawled, "You are going to need protection on your journey home this evening. You are sure to be accosted by a dozen love-smitten men. Allow me to offer my services as a guard."

The mixture of suggestiveness and amusement in

143

his voice made her stiffen. Cornelia felt just self-conscious enough to take offense. "I already have a man for protection, thank you, milord," she replied shortly.

"Bettonbrook?" he asked with what sounded like a trace of hostility.

"No. Margaret's brother is visiting us."

The earl's eyebrow went up. "A man is staying with you?"

"He is a vicar."

"He is still a man." Lord Taveston passed a significant look over her gown. This time his gaze did linger on her chest.

"I have his spinster sister for a chaperon, milord. Everything is altogether proper. Besides," she added with a sniff, "the vicar does not look at me the way some men do."

Lord Taveston's silky smile was full of insinuation. "And how is that?"

Goaded, she replied, "Like a predator."

"You must allow me to apologize for my sex. I am persuaded the men do not mean to look at you with anything but the most virtuous and innocent of eyes. It is only that in that gown you awaken something in men that is, ah . . . How to put this delicately?"

"Pray do not trouble yourself to find the word, milord." Cornelia swept up her skirts haughtily. "If you will excuse me, I have the next set promised." As she walked away she was aware he was watching her. Try as she might, she could not prevent her hips from swaying slightly or her gown from moving when she did. A true gentleman would not have noticed such things. She was absolutely certain that Lord Taveston was noticing.

Margaret rose from her chair next to the fire and touched Cornelia's arm. "Whatever is the matter? You look as if you have been insulted."

Cornelia glanced back at the earl and Margaret followed her gaze.

"Did Lord Taveston say something to overset you?" her friend asked.

Flustered, Cornelia ran a hand through her hair, disturbing the blue satin band woven through her curls. "It was not so much what he said as the way he said it."

Margaret cast a speculative look at Cornelia, then one back at Lord Taveston. "You must pay not the least mind to anything he says. He's a terrible fop." She continued to stare at him. "I am certain I have known him before, but I cannot recall where I met him."

Cornelia glared at the earl. It would serve him right if she broke her silence and told Margaret that he had been at the fair, Cornelia thought. Reason intervened. She could not allow her anger with him to put anyone in jeopardy.

Still, she remained annoyed with Lord Taveston. If he noted her uncharitable feelings toward him, they did not perturb him. Certainly they did not prevent him from joining the conversation when Lord Bettonbrook and the vicar were talking.

"I know your family distantly," the marquis said. "My aunt lives near Dunsmore."

"Yes, I knew her when I was young."

"Do any of your family still live there?"

"My parents."

"What of the other children?" Bettonbrook asked in an obvious attempt to keep the conversation alive.

"There's only Margaret and I."

"Ah."

Walter managed well enough at small country gatherings but he really was tongue-tied at larger social events, Cornelia thought as everyone fell silent. He was best when talking with one person. He had been very kind and understanding after Frederick's death and had talked to her at length offering consolation and the chance to unburden herself.

"How is your dear aunt?" Margaret smoothly interjected.

"Well enough for a woman of her age."

"She was always so sweet."

Walter faded into the background where he seemed most comfortable.

Still, Cornelia noted in his favor, he was solicitous and gentlemanly in seeking out plump girls or those with pock-marked faces and graciously escorted them out onto the floor. If he was not such a good dancer, at least he made the effort.

Lord Taveston escorted Margaret out for a set.

Lord Bettonbrook watched him depart with an expression of distaste. Then he turned to her. "Will you be receiving callers tomorrow?"

What an odd question. She was home every morning to callers. "Yes."

He cleared his throat. "I would like to visit you tomorrow. I have, er, something I wish to discuss." He tugged at his cravat.

Cornelia nodded. She could think of only one reason for his nervousness. Thinking about what that was made her agitated. It also gave her food for reflection, and she was distracted throughout the rest of the evening.

She roused herself on the way home to make polite conversation with Margaret and Walter.

"Did you enjoy yourself at your first London fete?" Cornelia asked Walter. The lights on the side of the carriage cast a pale glow inside, and she could see the pair seated across from her.

"It was pleasant," he said politely. "I am accustomed to the slower pace of country life, and I doubt I shall attend many soirees. But it was kind of you to include me in your invitation."

"Walter spends most of his evenings preparing his sermons and reading from the scripture," Margaret explained. "He is not so frivolous as I."

"You are not frivolous," Cornelia objected. "You simply like to go out and enjoy yourself." Walter, kind and good though he was, had not been as adept as his sister at talking with people. When he was not dancing with plain girls, she had noticed that he spent much of his time silently watching others.

"Never mind," Margaret said. "In the morning I shall show Walter the sights of London."

"Yes." Cornelia turned and looked out the window at the rows of townhouses they were passing. Her own plans for tomorrow were also set. Lord Bettonbrook was surely going to offer for her. The moment she had anticipated was about to arrive. What would she say if he asked her to marry him?

The next morning Cornelia was in her sitting room when she received word her stable hand Robert was waiting to speak with her in the kitchen.

Robert was laughing with Sally, the pretty young cook, when Cornelia entered the room. The pair immediately fell silent. Sally turned back to the stove and Robert began examining his well-worn boots.

"You wished to see me, Robert?"

"Aye." He began working the rim of his hat with coarse fingers. "Someone took the horse out again. About three in the morning it was. This time I got a glimpse," he added proudly.

"Who was it?"

"That I can't say. It was dark, but I know that it was a woman."

"A woman?" she repeated in surprise.

"A good rider at that. 'Twas the new horse I'm still trying to tame to the saddle. It's a very spirited horse."

Cornelia sat on the wooden bench and leaned back against the cool stone wall. What woman would take a half-wild horse out into the night streets of London? "Could you tell anything about her?"

Robert squinted in thought. "She was not tall, not short. She had a cloak over her. I couldn't see much."

"Then how can you be sure it was a woman?"

He colored and glanced toward the cook. "It was in the way that she walked, if you take my meaning."

"Yes, I do." Cornelia thought of her own walk last night when she had been certain Lord Taveston's eyes were on her.

In the calm reason of daylight, she wondered if she had not invited such a look with her clinging gown and exposed bosom. Then was it not missish to be offended by his frank male notice? She should be honest enough to admit that she had wanted him to look at her the same way he had looked at Lady

148

Jane. Cornelia shook her head, confused by her conflicting thoughts.

"Did I say something wrong?" Robert asked.

"No." Roused back to the matter at hand, she said, "I shall speak with the indoor staff today and try to discover if it was any of them. I would ask that you interview Jack in the stables."

"Yes, ma'am."

Cornelia dismissed Robert.

Wearily, she glanced around the kitchen. She might as well begin with the help here.

"Sally, would you come here a moment?"

The cook approached, dusting her floured hands on her apron.

"Sit down, please. I'm sure you overheard my conversation with Robert."

"I never listen to other people's talk," Sally informed her loftily. "However, I did happen to overhear a snippet. I didn't take the horse out."

"Do you know anyone who might have?"

Sally shook her head.

"Are any of the servants unhappy?"

"No, ma'am. Most of them like it well enough here. The upstairs maid sometimes complains that the house is not as grand as where she used to work, but she can barely ride a pony, let alone a horse."

"I see. Thank you." She hoped talking with the other servants revealed more.

Alas, it was not to be. Cornelia spent the next two hours talking to the servants. Her questions were met with varying degrees of outrage, curiosity, and denial. No one knew anything.

"Well someone is leaving this house," Cornelia muttered to herself as she trekked out to the stables later that afternoon to talk to Robert. She found him putting out hay for the horses. "Did Jack know anything?"

He leaned on the pitchfork and shook his head. "No. He sleeps in the loft near me. I would have heard if he had gotten up in the night. Since he was with the master the night he got shot, poor Jack is afraid to be in the dark by himself."

Cornelia nodded. "If someone takes a horse out again, you are to notify me immediately. I don't care what time of night it is."

"Wake you up, ma'am?"

"Yes."

She went back to the house, still preoccupied with the question of the horse. Lord Bettonbrook was waiting for her.

He was pacing the parlor when she entered. He stopped and looked at her solemnly.

She nodded to him and felt the tension creeping into her shoulders.

His reply was a barely audible murmur.

"Would you like some tea?" She moved toward the rope to ring for it.

"No, I wish to speak to you alone." Having delivered this bit of news, he fell silent and paced first to the window, then to the fireplace.

Cornelia eased into an overstuffed chair, feeling nerveless. He was going to ask her to marry him. She could tell by the look of concentration and uncertainty on his face. He kept tugging at his waistcoat and pausing to check his watch.

"Would you like to sit down?" she suggested.

He sat down across from her on the edge of the chair. "Lady Devenish—Cornelia, I have long admired your superior intellect and your calm reason. These qualities make you a good mother to Elizabeth, and I am persuaded they made you a good wife to Sir Frederick." He began to clear his throat and got lost in a cough.

Cornelia waited with rising anxiety.

Recovering, he continued, "I am sure the marked attention I have paid you has not been lost on you." Again he paused.

"Indeed it has not," she replied, but he seemed not to hear her.

"I know there is a difference in our ages, but I find you mature beyond your years."

She waited. He coughed, looked around the room, and then drew a deep breath. "I have come to ask you—"

Just then the parlor door opened and the maid stepped in. "You have another visitor."

Both Lord Bettonbrook and Cornelia turned toward the door as Lord Taveston entered. He looked fastidiously turned out in a white coat and black pantaloons that blended perfectly with his black Hessians, Cornelia noted absently.

Cornelia was vaguely aware the earl was making polite opening remarks. Hadn't he just commented on the weather? "The weather is very fine," she replied.

He looked at her oddly. Perhaps he had inquired after her health.

Lord Bettonbrook rose abruptly. He cast an annihilating look at the earl and said brusquely, "If you will excuse me, I will take my leave."

Lord Taveston glanced from one to the other. The door closed behind Cornelia's suitor and she bit back a sigh. The earl, having never been invited to sit down, still stood by the door.

"I interrupted at a bad time, didn't I?" he asked bluntly.

"Well . . ."

"He was asking you to marry him." It was a statement, not a question.

Cornelia said nothing.

"Were you going to accept him?"

She rose in agitation. "Whatever I decide to do is between myself and Lord Bettonbrook."

"Cornelia, be reasonable. You don't seriously want to marry him."

Angered, she challenged, "Why not?"

"Because he is dull and old."

Her ire increased. The fact she did not find the marquis fascinating only made the point more sore. "I like Lord Bettonbrook very well. At any rate," she added sharply, "I am no longer so naive as to expect the same things from marriage I once did."

"When I first met you, you spoke highly of Frederick," he reminded her.

"That was before I knew the truth," she snapped.

"Just because Frederick didn't tell you everything does not alter what was good about your marriage. Frederick considered the good of other people. Don't selfishly think only of yourself."

"You have no right to come here and talk to me this way."

"Neither have you the right to tarnish the memory of a good man with your resentments," he replied coldly.

She had heard all that she intended to stay and listen to. "I trust you have unburdened yourself sufficiently, milord. If you are quite through, I am leaving." Spinning on her heel, she stalked out of the room.

Cornelia fumed for a good hour before she calmed down enough to wonder how the earl could upset her so much. She recalled having been this angry when she had had lover's quarrels with Frederick. But few had awakened the same high pitch of emotion in her.

Chapter 10

He was twice a fool, Edwin cursed himself as he sat with his long legs stretched toward the fire and a glass of brandy at his elbow. He thought it was his third glass but it might have been his fourth. He heard his study door open and looked up to see Linton slide into the room. The viscount was good at entering and leaving houses unobtrusively; it came with the type of work he did.

"Did you go to see Frederick's widow?" Linton asked.

"Yes."

"Was she able to enlighten you further about what she had seen in the Hauserman's library?"

Edwin twisted his lips ironically. "I don't know if she could have or not. I did not get that far. I had intended to soften her with an apology for my ungentlemanly behavior toward her the other night."

Linton looked at him curiously. "What did you do that was ungentlemanly?"

"It doesn't signify." Sinking lower in the overstuffed chair, Edwin took another sip of brandy. "As soon as I saw her and Bettonbrook acting so peculiar today I should have left. But I stayed and made a bad situation worse by asking her whether she intended to accept Bettonbrook." He reached for the bottle. Well, dammit, *was* she going to accept him? "The man is much too old for her and stiff-necked into the bargain. A woman of sense would realize that."

Linton watched him askance. "What has all this to say to getting information from her? You don't care if she is seeing another man. All you want from her is to find out what she knows."

"Of course." Edwin recalled with regret that he had also upbraided Cornelia for the resentment she had come to feel toward Frederick. He could not have made a greater mull of the situation if he had tried. And Linton was right. Why did he care? It was nothing to him if she married Bettonbrook. His interest in her was in gaining information. Wasn't it?

No, he admitted with an audible sigh. He had a far greater interest in her. Else why had he twice driven by her house yesterday when another route home would have been faster?

His personal feelings did not matter, though. The work of the Crown deserved his first attention. He believed she was not indifferent to him, but she had been too hurt by Frederick to make another match based on feelings. She was certain to marry Lord Bettonbrook precisely because he did not stir her emotions. Edwin was powerless to change that. All he could do was throw his full attention to his work for his country.

"I have to go back to see her," he said tiredly. "This time my apology must be very winning."

He fortified himself with another sip of brandy before rising.

"You haven't formed an attachment for Frederick's widow, have you, Edwin?" Linton asked with a frown.

"No."

Linton looked relieved.

"I shall straighten out this coil," he said with brisk purpose. "When I return, we must discuss getting someone into the Hauserman house in the capacity of a maid or a butler. There's something havey-cavey going on there, and we must get to the bottom of it."

"Cornelia, if Lord Bettonbrook meant to ask you to marry him, he will certainly return," Margaret said.

"Yes, of course." Cornelia managed a faint smile at Margaret and Walter.

The three of them were sitting in the breakfast room enjoying a light luncheon. At least the other two were eating. She had little appetite. Her mind was too full of the morning's events. First there had been Lord Bettonbrook's near proposal and then Lord Taveston's unforgivable behavior. A gentleman would not have quizzed her about her intentions toward the marquis. Neither would he have brought up Frederick's name or discussed her memory of him.

"Is something else weighing on your mind?" Walter asked.

He was very perceptive, Cornelia thought.

"If you wish to talk to us or to me, I should be glad to listen. I am a vicar," he added solemnly. "I am not unused to helping people with their problems."

"I appreciate your offer."

Margaret was not so reticent. "Give over, Cornelia. You're among friends. If something has overset you, tell us."

"Well," she began slowly. "I am not certain why Lord Taveston came to see me. He became rather ... direct and asked me outright if Lord Bettonbrook had proposed. He also mentioned Frederick."

"Frederick? Did Lord Taveston know him?" Margaret asked.

"Yes, I believe so." Belatedly remembering that he had asked her to keep his secret, she fell silent.

"How did Taveston know your husband?"

"They were at Eton together many years ago." Cornelia left off the part about Frederick giving Edwin her locket and about Edwin's appearance at the fair.

"I see." Margaret glanced toward her brother. After a moment, she asked, "Do you wish Walter to speak to Lord Taveston? If you feel the earl has acted improperly toward you or made statements that call your character into question, then I am sure Walter would defend your honor by—"

"No, no," Cornelia demurred. The idea of Walter calling the earl out did not bear thinking about. She knew immediately who the loser in such a contest would be. Without ever having seen the earl fire a gun, she knew that he would be steady and deadly. Walter would not stand a chance.

Margaret continued to look at her with concern. "You still seem unhappy. Is that all that happened? Is there more you are not telling us?"

"No. There is nothing more."

Walter picked up his teacup. "We must not pry, Margaret. Cornelia is entitled to keep her thoughts to herself if she wishes."

"I am always inclined to be too inquisitive," Margaret admitted. "Even when Walter and I were children, I was always asking questions."

"Children can be like that," Cornelia said, leaping on the chance to change the subject. "I am persuaded Elizabeth will be full of questions when she is older."

"She's such a bright child," Margaret agreed.

"Yes." Cornelia started to launch into an anecdote about Elizabeth but stopped herself. She laughed shortly. "I never thought I would be one of those mothers who repeats every precious thing her daughter says. But Elizabeth's actions are so dear I often find myself relating them to others."

"I think that's part of being a mother," Walter said mildly.

Cornelia thought about the last such cute incident she had told to Lord Bettonbrook and how he had merely nodded. Of course she should not expect everyone to take the interest in her daughter that she did, but if she were to marry the marquis, she would wish him to be greatly concerned with Elizabeth.

The other woman pushed back her chair. "If you will excuse me, I have some letters to write."

Walter rose also. "Yes, and I must work on a sermon I have been asked to give this Sunday."

"Here in London?" Cornelia asked politely.

"It's a small parish just south of the city. I know the vicar there. I shall go for the whole of the weekend." He smiled. "You two shall have the house to yourselves again."

"We enjoy having you," Margaret insisted.

"Indeed we do," Cornelia agreed.

Brother and sister left the room together.

Cornelia remained a few moments longer. She was just rising from the table when the maid appeared. "Lord Taveston, milady." The maid's voice betrayed curiosity. After all, the earl had called but three hours ago, and now he was back. That was most unusual.

"Thank you," Cornelia said and set her jaw firmly. He had a great deal of nerve to return after what he had said to her earlier. Did he think because she was without a husband or man to protect her that she must suffer whatever insults he wished to hurl?

Fueled with anger, she strode to the parlor. The earl was waiting by the fireplace. She stood with her hand on the doorknob facing him in cold silence.

He smiled ruefully. "You needn't hover there, Cornelia. I won't bite if you come in."

She refused to be so susceptible to his smile, however winsome it might be.

"I have returned to ask that you overlook my churlish behavior of this morning," he said. "I had no right to question you concerning Lord Bettonbrook."

"No, you had no right." She kept her back straight and her head up.

"I acted without thinking. Everyone does so from time to time. I am painfully aware I brought up subjects which I had no right to broach." His head was bowed repentantly.

"You did not have a right," she agreed.

"I should not have made any mention of Frederick."

"You should not have done." It was growing more difficult to maintain a rigid demeanor at the sight of Lord Taveston being so accommodating and apologetic. The meekness was uncharacteristic of him. That, coupled with her relief that they were not going to continue to argue, softened her.

"Did I do anything else to offend you this morning?" he asked gravely.

She frowned. "I do not recall that you spit on the floor or cleaned your boots on the table."

"No, I don't think even I did that. Are you laughing at me, Cornelia?" He stepped nearer.

"A bit," she admitted. "I'm sorry. I should not do so, but seeing you so contrite confuses me."

"I daresay that making sport of me is better than throwing me from the house."

Cornelia tried but failed to imagine herself putting the well-muscled earl out the door if he did not want to go. She could not conceive of anyone forcing Lord Taveston to do anything he didn't wish to do.

"I could make you a lot of pretty speeches, but I'll not insult your intelligence with such obvious ploys. I came this morning because I wanted something from you. I have returned because I still want it." He looked steadily at her.

Had she really thought all those apologies were for no purpose? He wanted something from her.

"I need to know what you saw the night you went to the Hauserman's library." He sat down across from her and leaned forward in his chair, his hands clasped together in front of him, his eyes fixed on her.

His cravat was still impeccably tied, she noted, but his hair was no longer so smoothly in place as it had been this morning. Unless she was mistaken she smelled brandy on his breath.

"Any details you can give might help."

She remembered many details from that night. She recalled opening the door of the library and flying into the unyielding length of the earl's body. She recalled his strong arms wrapping around her to steady her. But those were probably not the details he wanted.

"What caused you to go into the library?" he asked. "Had you heard a noise?"

"No." She hesitated. She had no reason not to tell him about the man in the opera hat. The truth was she had given the matter little thought. Something about the man had struck her as familiar, but she never had been able to place him.

"I was standing in the hall," she began slowly, "looking out over the area where the carriages were kept. I saw two men talking. Both men were in the shadows. They caught my attention because they seemed very secretive. When they parted, I went into the library to see if I could get a closer look at the man in the hat as he went around the side of the house. That's when I was surprised by someone in the library."

"Why did you want to get a closer look?"

"Because he's someone I know or that I have met, but I can't remember who."

Lord Taveston sat back in the chair and continued to watch her. "Can you even make a guess who the man was?"

She shook her head. "I'm sorry."

"Was he tall or short?"

"Medium, I should imagine. Maybe a little tall."

"Heavy?"

She shook her head. "I cannot say. It was dark. There are few specifics I can recall, only that something about him seemed familiar."

Rising, he paced to the fireplace and whisked a hand through his hair. "Was it the way he stood or walked or what he wore that seemed familiar?"

She closed her eyes and concentrated. "It must have been the way he was standing, for I noticed him before I ever saw him take a step."

Opening her eyes, she saw the earl nodding at her in encouragement to continue. She spread her hands. "That's all I can recall."

"I see." He was clearly disappointed. "You will promise to keep trying to remember."

"Yes."

Straightening, he bowed, but he did not go. She thought he seemed reluctant to take his leave.

His lingering gave her the courage to say something that was on her mind for some time. "Lord Taveston, I know that these are dangerous times. I hope that you are being careful."

He inclined his head in surprise.

She colored. "What I am trying to say is I know the work that you do can lead you into danger. I hope you take no chances and that that no harm comes to you."

"Thank you, Cornelia" he said slowly.

The hall clock sounded and for the space of all four rings, they stood and looked at each other. Under his intense green gaze, she felt suddenly shy. She didn't know what to do with her hands or where to direct her gaze.

The silence between them felt heavy with unsaid words. Yet when she began to talk to fill up the silence, she said silly things. "I miss the country somewhat. The people here are very nice, but parties begin to grow old after a time. The air is not so fresh in London."

He treated her babbling as if it were intelligent conversation. "I wondered if you would begin to pine for the country. You grew up there, did you not?"

"Yes. I have been to Bath and Brighton several times, but it is not the same as the frantic pace of London."

"I have a sister who lives in Bath."

"Do you? How many are in your family, milord?"

"Two girls. I'm the only son."

"I recollect you said once that you are an uncle."

He nodded.

This was the sort of idle chatter she and Lord Taveston had never shared together. As he named off his nieces and nephews, she listened to the rise and fall of his voice. She found the deep resonance of his words soothing. Where the sun coming in through the window touched the crown of his head, the hairs glinted golden.

"When will you return to Devon?" he was asking.

"In a little over two weeks. I must begin preparing for the fair as soon as I return." She smiled. "I should start working on my speech and practicing it in front of my mirror as soon as possible. I would like to be more polished this time."

"I think you did well last year. You were a bit nervous," he admitted, "but you sounded sincere. Few women would have given the speech at all. I admire you for doing so."

"Thank you." His praise pleased her enormously.

She noted with regret that he was looking toward the clock. "Would you like some tea?" she suggested to forestall his leaving.

"Thank you, but I must go."

"Of course."

After he left, the rest of her day was full. She had menus to plan and invitations to respond to. She had promised to take Elizabeth out for a ride in the carriage. She also tried hard to think about the man in the opera hat, but her mind remained blank. Mostly, though, her thoughts kept returning to things she and Lord Taveston had said to each other.

She was still reworking the conversation when she went to bed that evening. In her mind she came up with brilliant repartee and lyrical responses to his statements. She thought back to those moments while the clock chimed and they had looked at each other in silence. It had felt as if they were more than two people who were loosely acquainted. But he had not been there as a suitor, she reminded herself.

Still, she fell to sleep thinking about Lord Taveston instead of about Lord Bettonbrook's near proposal.

She was fast asleep when she heard voices.

At first she thought they were part of her dream, but they rose and fell in volume. Blinking groggily, she raised up on her elbow and heard someone talking. Still not fully awake, she stumbled out of bed, reached for a wrapper, and threw it over her shoulders.

Was that Margaret speaking?

Barefoot, Cornelia followed the sound out her door and down the hall to the room next to hers. Outside the door, she paused and listened. She was wide awake now. The voices were not those of fear but of anger, she realized. Margaret was shrieking and a man was trying to soothe her.

"We have to do something. We can't just let things go along as they are," Margaret said

The man's voice was too low to distinguish the words.

Cornelia hesitated. It was not her style to stand outside people's bedroom doors and listen. Still, she could not help wondering what a man was doing in Margaret's room at this hour of the night.

The man spoke again and this time she could make out parts of his sentence.

". . . taking chances . . . the location must be right . . . carefully planned."

It was Walter. Cornelia took a step back from the door, trying to step lightly so the floor didn't creak. The pair inside the room must have fallen into a calmer conversation for all she could hear now were muffled words.

Turning, she crept back to her own room. It was surprising for Walter to be in his sister's bedroom in the middle of the night, but Cornelia was certainly not going to intrude.

She returned to her own bed and tried to go back to sleep. Margaret had been so anxious for Walter to come to London, and the pair always seemed to get along so well that tonight's noisy disagreement startled Cornelia.

Perhaps they were not so close as she had thought. A disturbing thought came to her that they were not really brother and sister. After all, Lord Bettonbrook had said that a boy had been adopted, and later on she had learned there were only Margaret and Walter in the family, so Walter had to be the boy who was adopted. That being the case, it was not entirely proper for them to be in a bedroom together. But that was splitting hairs,

165

Cornelia told herself. They had been raised together since the time Walter was ten years old. Surely that made them like blood kin.

She searched for a comfortable spot on the bed and tried to go back to sleep.

Chapter 11

"She will be ready for a pony soon, Cornelia," Margaret observed as Elizabeth rocked her hobby horse. The two women were idly working on samplers while Elizabeth played in the corner of the parlor.

"Dear me, I am not prepared to think of her on a horse yet."

"Why not? I had one by the time I was two. A child must learn early if she is to become an accomplished horsewoman."

"I did not have a horse until I was five," Cornelia said.

"That's too late."

Cornelia glanced at Margaret and then carefully took a stitch. "You must be a very good rider."

"I used to be. At one time I could jump a five-barred gate."

"They say you never lose that ability." A vague idea at the back of Cornelia's mind took bolder shape. Robert had said a woman had taken the horse out. He had also said it had been a half-tamed horse of great spirit. It would take someone very good to control such an animal. Margaret? And if

167

so, did her midnight rides somehow figure into her argument with Walter

Margaret shrugged. "Perhaps not. I don't know. I rarely ride these days."

"I see."

Cornelia's mind continued to spin possibilities. Walter might have found out Margaret was going out at night and that had caused the argument last night. What reasons could there be for going abroad alone at such a late hour? Memories of Margaret's words about passion led Cornelia to speculate there might be a man involved. If so, she was willing to bet he was singularly inappropriate to Margaret's station as a vicar's sister.

Suddenly conscious that talk between them had died, Cornelia said, "I hope all goes well for Walter this weekend."

"What do you mean?"

"I hope his sermon is well received."

"Oh, yes, of course."

Cornelia looked up to find her companion watching her. Their eyes met and held. She decided on frankness. "Is something wrong, Margaret? I know you and your brother quarreled last night. I should be glad to listen if there is anything you wish to discuss with me."

"It was a family matter," the other woman said tersely. "We have resolved it." She changed the subject. "I understand Lord Taveston called on you twice the other day."

"Yes." Cornelia concentrated again on her stitches and silently cursed the servants for gossiping.

"It sounds as if he is courting you."

"No, he is not."

"Why else would a man come to see a woman twice in the same day?"

"He had something he wished to discuss with me."

"Nothing of a romantic nature?"

"No."

They both fell silent, neither having given the other the information she sought. Tension hung in the air. Even Elizabeth must have felt it, for she stopped rocking and came over to whine and pull at Cornelia's skirts.

"Have you heard from Lord Bettonbrook again?" Margaret asked.

Cornelia shook her head. She recalled his dark look when Lord Taveston had interrupted his proposal. He was angry and suspicious of the earl, Cornelia realized. Unless she made an effort to smooth things over, she did not think he would return.

Elizabeth continued to fuss.

"She is tired," Cornelia said. "I'll take her up to bed."

She was thankful for the opportunity to escape. Little bits of information kept floating around in her mind. They didn't amount to anything concrete, but they were troublesome nonetheless. Why was Margaret always asking about Lord Taveston? He seemed to be of great interest to her. Then there was the matter of the horse being taken out at unreasonable hours, and there was the quarrel between Margaret and her soft-spoken brother.

No doubt she was letting her imagination run away with her, Cornelia thought. The only thing that ought to really concern her was contacting Lord Bettonbrook. Yet she did not sit down at her desk and write to him.

It was after two in the morning when Lord Taveston returned from White's. His valet was snoring in the dressing room, and he didn't bother to rouse him. The earl was shrugging out of his shirt when he heard a knock downstairs.

Who would come to the front door at this hour? Linton and Natale and any of the others who might call at this late hour would do so at the back door.

Buttoning his shirt, he went down the stairs. He opened the door and Margaret Simpson rushed in.

"You must come quickly," she said frantically. "Cornelia is gone. She was called out to tend a sick man hours ago, and she has not returned."

"Do you know where she went?"

"One of the servants told me the direction, but I don't know where it is." She thrust a crumpled piece of paper toward him and he read the direction written in a scrawled hand.

"Good Lord, this is one of the worse parts of London. No woman could go there alone."

"She is not alone. She has a driver with her."

"That's scarcely any better. They are venturing into a den of thieves and cutthroats." Grabbing his coat, he slung it over his shoulders and started toward the back door for the stables.

She clutched at his arm. "I'll go with you."

"This is no place for you." Besides, he didn't want her slowing him down. "Go back home."

"You must take me. I won't have a moment's peace until I know she is safe."

"I'll send word." Without giving Margaret Simpson a backward glance, he disappeared out the back door. Seconds later he took off riding furiously down the cobblestone street.

Cornelia was fast asleep when she heard the pounding on her door. She roused quickly. "Who is it?"

"Robert, ma'am."

She could not see a clock, but it felt very late. Someone must be ill for him to awaken her at this hour.

He quickly gave the lie to that notion. "Someone has taken a horse out. I woke up to find it gone," he said through the closed door.

"I shall be out in a minute." She lit a candle, pulled off her nightgown and slipped into a heavy brown dress.

She had had just about enough of this nonsense of someone stealing a horse from her as if she were a public stables. This time, she was going to be there when the rider returned and was going to confront whoever was doing this.

She pulled on a pair of heavy shoes and opened the door. Robert stood in the hall holding a low-burning lantern near his hip.

"I'm sure the household is already awake." She paused at the door of Margaret's bedroom. No sound came from within. Cornelia had never discussed the matter of the horses being taken from the stables with Margaret, but now she considered waking her. Then she changed her mind. If Margaret could sleep through this, she would not disturb her.

Robert was already going down the steps. Cornelia hurried after him. They crossed the empty

171

yard behind the house toward the hulking black outline that was the stable. She had just entered through the front door when a horse and rider surged out the back door.

Cornelia saw a blur of dark forms and heard the clatter of hooves.

"Dammit," Robert expostulated. They've taken a second horse."

Her anger rose even high. The problem was even getting worse, for now two horses were gone. Whoever was doing this was going to be punished. First, though, she must find out who it was. Until this minute, she had intended to wait for the person's return. Now, she was too agitated to sit and wait.

"We are going after them, Robert."

He stared at her in the murky light from the lantern. "Beggin' your pardon, ma'am, but by the time I get two horses saddled, whoever 'twas will be long gone."

"We're not going to saddle the horses. Riding bareback is not what I do best, but I can manage," she said through gritted teeth. Without regard to ladylike decorum, she climbed into the stall and began untying a horse.

"Are you sure—"

"Help me on the horse, Robert."

A startled Robert obliged and then pulled onto the back of another horse. Cornelia ducked her head on her way out the back door.

Robert was right behind her. "I think I see him far up ahead."

She gave the horse its head once they were in the open.

Robert soon pulled ahead of her. He was faster

and more adept at riding than she but determination helped make up for what Cornelia lacked in skill. She held onto the mare's bare mane and followed the stable hand.

The night air was cold, and low-lying fog swirled like water around them. Ignoring that, Cornelia bent low and concentrated on staying with the horse. Her unbound hair flew back behind her and her skirts flapped with the wind.

The horseman ahead of them raced down darkened streets and turned corners onto even darker streets. A time or two Robert and Margaret lost him, but each time they stopped and listened for the fading sound of hoofbeats and were able to steer themselves in the right direction again.

Cornelia soon lost all sense of direction. They rode for what seemed a long time. She fell further behind Robert. Eventually she was only following him and not the person who had stolen the horse.

The wide, spacious streets of Mayfair gave way to an area where smaller houses were crowded closer together. The empty streets still maintained an air of genteel respectability. As they continued to ride, that changed too. Soon Cornelia found herself riding down narrow, winding roads that wrapped around buildings and emerged into tiny greens before plunging back into crowded streets.

She and Robert journeyed further into the congested area. The streets were no longer deserted as they had been in her respectable neighborhood. Here drunks stood in the roadway and shouted to each other or to no one. Women leaned against lampposts in suggestive poses. Through the open door of pubs and gin houses, she heard raucous laughter.

Horsemen racing through at this time of night were obviously not so great a curiosity here as they would have been elsewhere. Still, the sight of a woman did arouse brief interest and the occasional lewd comment was thrown after her. Cornelia was too intent on following Robert to listen or care.

She was more concerned about the nip of the wind and the smell of stout and old rags and rotting fish that draped over the whole area like a nauseating vapor.

Who of her servants was coming to this wretched part of town and why?

As they rode out of the area of gin houses and into a section of bleak-looking tenement dwellings, Robert reined in and dropped back to her side. "We should go back. A lady like yourself should not be here."

"No."

He cleared his throat to argue.

"The area cannot get any worse." Besides, the chase was in her blood now. Even the horse seemed caught up in it and pawed the ground restlessly while they talked.

She peered into the distance but saw only darkness punctuated by the occasional lamplight. "Have we lost him?" she asked anxiously.

"I can make him out far ahead. He still doesn't know we are back here." Robert gazed hard, then muttered, "He stopped. He's getting off his mount and going into a building."

This was good news. "We can get up closer and wait outside until he comes back out." Cornelia did not think he would be inside long. The horses were always returned to the stables long before daylight, so whoever took them out did not linger long wherever he went.

When they were within a block of the house, Robert slid down and helped her alight. They tied their horses to a decaying post.

"You wait here. I'll get up closer and see if I can see anythin' through the window."

Cornelia did as he commanded. While Robert crept along the front of buildings, keeping well in their shadows, she hugged herself against the night chill. Now that he was not by her side, she began to have her first doubts about her mission. Robert was right: this was no area for her. Why had she not waited at the stables for the horses to be returned? But her outrage and curiosity had been too strong to allow her to sit there. Now that she was here, she was going to see the matter through.

Robert reached the building and disappeared around the side of it.

Alone, Cornelia shrank deeper into the shadows. She heard the loud panting of her horse. Somewhere a baby cried. Further away a man and woman screamed at each other. A dog barked.

She waited. And waited. Still Robert did not return. With an increasing sense of unease, she looked around her. Her eyes were growing accustomed to the darkness. Behind her she could make out the dark shape of a door. Turning back toward the building, she willed Robert to return.

Suddenly someone touched her from behind. Her scream was silenced by a heavy hand over her mouth.

"Don't make a sound," a man growled.

She stood frozen.

"Do you understand me?"

Terrified, she nodded.

The hand was slowly withdrawn. She stood petrified.

"Turn around."

She obeyed, moving woodenly. The figure that loomed over her was instantly familiar even in the murkiness. "L-Lord Taveston."

"At your service," he said with grim sarcasm.

Something glinted in his hand. She looked down to see a gun he held pointed directly at her. She began to shake all over.

"I have already tied up your servant behind the house so do not expect help from him. Now I want you to go in there and tell your friends you were not able to lure me here."

"My friends?" Her voice was a quivering bleat.

"Fellow spies, if you wish to quibble about terms. Lord Hauserman and the Simpsons."

She looked back toward the house. "Margaret? Walter? They are in there?"

"Don't come the innocent with me, Cornelia. Oh, I do admit I was fooled for a long time. When Margaret came tonight saying you were missing, my first impulse was to rush out to look for you. I even got on my horse and started out. Then I began to think."

She wet her lips and looked fearfully down at the gun.

"Why would Margaret come to me instead of to Lord Bettonbrook?" Lord Taveston continued. "After all, he is your suitor. But you know the answer to that question as well as I. It was me they wanted, not Bettonbrook."

Cornelia shook her head numbly. Nothing made sense. If Margaret was meeting Lord Hauserman in an illicit tryst, why was the vicar here as well? That left only darker possibilities. Her mind flashed back to the night at the Hausermans when someone had been in the library with her. The door leading out of the room had been locked. It occurred to her for the first time that the master of the house would have had a key.

Lord Taveston had used the terms "spies." It seemed clear to her now that Lord Hauserman was a spy. And Margaret and the vicar? The midnight rides and late night quarrels took on a whole new meaning. So did Margaret's continuing interest in Lord Taveston. Her suspicion of him had been growing, and she had been watching his movements.

"Margaret may have tried to trap you," Cornelia said in a hoarse voice, "but I had nothing to do with it."

"Then why are you here waiting in the shadows?" The question was spoken in a reasonable voice but she detected harshness behind it. And something like pain.

"Someone took a horse from my stable. Robert and I followed him here."

"Do you want to know something amusing, Cornelia? Even now I want to believe you. I want to ignore the questions about why you were in the library and why Margaret Simpson was living with you. I want to believe you're innocent. But you see, my dear, the facts don't support that."

"I am innocent!"

Up the street the door of the house opened and a figure she recognized as Lord Hauserman emerged. The earl put a hand over her mouth and pulled her back against him. Tears of frustration stung at her eyes.

"He's not coming or he would have been here by now," Lord Hauserman said angrily.

Margaret ran out the door after him. "He may have gotten lost. He's coming. He believed me."

"I was afraid he was too smart for us. He probably went to Lady Devenish's house and found her at home and realized it was all a hoax." The furious Lord Hauserman climbed into the saddle of his waiting horse and rode away.

Walter emerged behind Margaret. She turned to him and lifted her hands in frustration. "He'll be here," she insisted in a voice that rose hysterically.

"Calm down." The vicar stroked her hair and kissed her forehead.

She leaned against him and whimpered.

His mouth found hers and lingered there. It was a very unbrotherly kiss.

The earl's hand fell away from Cornelia's mouth but she didn't move. She simply stared.

Walter drew back and talked to Margaret in reassuring accents. "Taveston has only eluded us for the moment, Margaret. We shall get him."

The pair fell into another embrace.

"Well, they're out of the house now," the earl muttered grimly and walked forward. The gun was on them instead of her. Drained, she waited in the shadows.

Margaret saw him first. "Walter!"

"How charming to see you, Miss Simpson. I hope it won't upset you unduly if my friend ties you up."

Cornelia watched as another man appeared from nowhere.

"Tie them securely, Linton. We wouldn't want them to get away."

"I thought you killed him," Margaret shrieked. "You said you had."

"Shut up, Margaret," Walter muttered.

"Once you have given this pair over to the authorities, see to Lord Hauserman," Lord Taveston directed Linton. "I have no doubt he has returned to his bed so there is no rush."

As Cornelia watched, the earl turned slowly and gazed down the street to where she stood. She stood motionless as he walked toward her. When he reached her, he gathered her into his arms.

Cornelia went without the least resistance. Smothered in the folds of his greatcoat, she closed her eyes and felt the comforting strength of his arms.

Cornelia had never actually seen the earl's house before because it sat behind a row of trees. Her first glimpse of the facade of glistening marble and graceful arching windows put her more in mind of a palace than a home. Inside, the halls were wide sweeps of black and white tile. Niches in the walls held statues.

But not all the rooms were so intimidating as the grand entryway. The walnut-paneled study Lord Taveston escorted her to smelled comfortably of the leather of old books. She found it very cozy seated next to the low-burning fire in his study.

She was not included in the meeting with the man Linton and several other people, but the earl asked her to wait for him. Lord Hauserman, Margaret, and Walter were also at the conference that was taking place behind closed doors in the formal-looking salon.

It was close to dawn when the salon door opened. Cornelia looked out into the hall and saw Edwin and his companions emerging with satisfied looks. Lord Hauserman and the Simpsons appearing grim and white-faced. As the trio was bundled down the hall, she saw that their hands were tied behind them.

The front door was out of her range of sight, but she heard murmured conversation and the sound of the door opening and closing several times. Finally, Lord Taveston walked back into the study.

The first pink lights of dawn were showing outside the window. Her hair was still an unsecured mane, and she wore the same clothes she had ridden in last night.

He stopped in the doorway. His smile stopped her heart for the space of two beats and took the breath from her.

"D-Did everything go well?" she asked.

"Yes. They were persuaded to divulge the names of other operators for Napoleon." His smile died. Looking very sober, he crossed the room and sat down beside her. "It was the vicar who shot Frederick, Cornelia."

It had been a night of too many shocks for one more to surprise her. "I guess that makes sense. After all, he lived in the area; it would not have been hard for him to find out my husband's movements."

"He may have been the one who knocked me out at the fair. I was lucky. He didn't realize who I was, or he would have finished me. But I must have gotten too close to where he was meeting with some others."

"Why would he do it?" Cornelia asked.

"His mother was French. He lived in France until he was nine. Then he was brought to this country and his mother died. The Simpsons took him in to raise, but his loyalty was always with his native country."

"He and Margaret were not really brother and sister," she murmured. She thought back to the scene she had overheard in the bedroom and realized their relationship had been that of lovers. "Margaret was in love with him; she would have done anything for him."

"I daresay that's true."

"He was also the man in the opera hat. I failed to recognize him because I was trying to think of someone I knew in society. He must have been in disguise at the time, but I recognized his walk." Her mind went back to a dozen little things, like how solicitous he and Margaret had been after Frederick's death and how they had encouraged her to talk.

"I don't understand why they tried to trap you tonight. If they had known all along who you were and what part you played in working for the Crown, why did they not kill you in Devon?"

"They didn't know then. Margaret had growing suspicions, I think, but she could not act alone. Once Walter was here, he may have learned something through his sources that decided him."

"Oh," she said in a small voice. He spoke so calmly about his life being in danger. Her knees still felt weak from the experience.

"It was Lord Hauserman you surprised in his

library," the earl said. "He must have been waiting for the vicar to come in, but your appearance ruined those plans. He had a key, though, so he could escape to a room where we could not follow."

"Yes," she murmured but her thoughts were less and less on the intrigue of spying and more on the way Lord Taveston was looking at her with such steady intensity.

She tried to smooth her disheveled hair with her restless fingers. "I must look a fright."

He shook his head wordlessly, his eyes never leaving her. The room felt choked with unsaid words.

Finally, he asked, "Cornelia, do you know Lord Bettonbrook's given name?"

She blinked at him, surprised by the question. "No, I don't."

"Do you think it advisable to marry without knowing a man's Christian name? Mine is Edwin," he added with the beginnings of the most appealing smile she had ever witnessed.

"I have not heard from Lord Bettonbrook since you interrupted his attempt to propose," she said. "I think he was jealous of you and believed there was something between you and I."

The earl considered that thoughtfully. "We could create something between you and I. I could call on you and bring flowers, and you could confide to your friends that you found my attentions not unwelcome." He slid closer to her on the sofa and took her hand. "Rumor might even begin to circulate that I had a score for you."

He stroked the back of her hand with slow, sensuous movements.

Even though her eyes were open, she felt the dreamy, floating sensation she associated with sleep. "Are you trying to seduce me, milord?"

"It's a thought. I'll stop if you want."

"No." She fitted herself more snugly against the contours of his body and closed her eyes. The touch of his mouth on her lips was not unexpected although the fierce passion of his kiss did take her momentarily aback. Then her own ardor rose up to meet his.

His kisses were full of romance and promise and persuasion. She felt the strength of his body and smelled the scent of port that clung to his lips. She liked all those things. In fact, she liked everything about him. By the time she finally emerged from his embrace, she was dazed and dazzled.

"I believe in long courtships," he said huskily. "With a special license we could be wed within three days. I think that plenty long enough for a courtship."

She was mute.

In the face of her silence, he hesitated. "You do not have any reservations, do you?"

"I could not abide the fact you would be in danger," she said softly, her emotions warring with her desire to accept him. But she could not lie. The thought that he would be in danger would eat at her.

"As to that, after tonight I could no longer work effectively for the Crown. Too many people know my part in this. I suppose I shall even give up the role of the dandy, although it may be the death of my valet." His teasing smile faded, and he was once again serious. "I know you were hurt by things you discovered after Frederick's death. Has that made you reluctant to ever marry for love again?"

"No." She was quite ready to take a chance and marry for love again. And again and again if it would make her feel such a wondrous glow.

"Then it is settled."

This time it was she who initiated the kiss.